Paulin........................ced author of eight
children's novels, including *Flying for Frankie*, *The Mrs
Marridge Project*, *Sabrina Fludde* and *Midnight Blue*
which won the Smarties Prize and was shortlisted for
the Whitbread Children's Book of the Year Award.
Pauline has five children and lives in Shropshire.

Praise for *Flying for Frankie*:

'Like almost everything she writes, it is a gem . . . It
is moving and heartwarming without being at all
sentimental.' *Observer*

Praise for *The Mrs Marridge Project*:

'Ingenious.' *Observer*

Praise for *Sabrina Fludde*:

'A multi-layered novel packed with big writing and
even bigger ideas.' *Guardian*

Praise for *Midnight Blue*, winner of the
Smarties Prize:

'Deeply satisfying . . . one of the year's best imagina-
tive novels.' *Sunday Times*

Praise for *Tyger Pool*:

'A brilliant novel that leaves its readers emotionally drained.' *Daily Telegraph*

Praise for *The Candle House*:

'This is a marvel.' *Observer*

www.paulinefisk.co.uk

IN THE TREES

PAULINE FISK

faber and faber

First published in 2010
by Faber and Faber Limited
Bloomsbury House, 74–77 Great Russell Street,
London WC1B 3DA

Typeset by Faber and Faber Limited
Printed in England by CPI Bookmarque, Croydon

A CIP record for this book
is available from the British Library

ISBN 978–0–571–23620–6

2 4 6 8 10 9 7 5 3 1

For Idris

'Sub Umbra Floreat'

('Under the Shade, I Flourish')
National Motto of Belize

PART ONE
SOUTH LONDON

1

KID'S CARDBOARD BOX

Ever since Nadine's text message, Kid had been in a hurry to get home. *Guess what*, it said. *It's here. Don't know where from, but it's on the doormat with your name on it! Kid Cato it says, and some other stuff which I can't read.*

Business was dead that night, which meant that Kid was able to take off the specials grill earlier than usual, transfer the quarter-pounders to the main grill and embark on what everybody in Jet's Burger Joint knew as 'the close' – that mysterious process by which machines were shut down and the establishment prepared for the following day.

If he could get through it all, Kid reckoned, then perhaps he'd be able to slip off even before the last customer was through the door. Maybe the floor would still need swabbing and the till cashing up, but those final things could be left to someone else.

Kid checked his mobile phone again. It was almost as if he couldn't quite believe what Nadine's message said. Jet gave him his special 'no phones at work' look, but he didn't care. He unclipped the Teflon clams, wiped them on both sides, pulled on a pair of rubber gloves and started attacking the grill with squeegee, scraper and a stack of cloths.

Under normal circumstances, Kid liked cleaning grills. It was the one job that everybody else hated, but he liked the uniformity of it. Liked the fact that, once you'd got the hang of it, you didn't need to think. But then Kid liked hard work. On a good night, he'd have the floor swept and the cashing-up done before the last customer disappeared and the sign went up on the door. The knack was not to get dragged into helping with any last-minute cooking, otherwise everything would have to start all over again.

But not tonight, Kid thought, dragging the scraper back and forth until the grill was shining. Please God, not tonight. He finished off the second grill and peeled off his gloves.

'That's it, boys and girls,' said Jet. 'Shut the door and pull down the blinds. No one else comes in. We're off.'

Kid didn't need to be told twice. He headed for the door. 'Hey, you slacker – have you put the buns out by the toasters?' Jet called after him.

'Yes,' Kid called back.

'Have the pots all been returned to their stations?'

'Yes.'

'Are you bloody perfect?' Jet called. 'Yes, *of course* you are! Get out of here – I don't want to see your ugly face again until tomorrow night. Six on the dot, or else you're fired!'

Kid knew Jet would never fire him. Who else was going to do what he did for the pittance he was paid? Sometimes it really got to him how mean Jet was and he'd go home grumbling. But tonight he headed off into the south London night with better things on his mind.

The streets were still busy, even though it was late. Horns honked as he ducked and dived his way across roads, and late-night revellers swore as he pushed past them on the pavement. Leaving the main roads behind, he ducked into a network of back streets and alleys, taking a short cut up and down a couple of fire escapes and ending up at the top-floor flat where he was living these days with Nadine, his mother's ex-boyfriend's half-sister.

Usually when Kid came in, the flat would be in darkness and Nadine would be out somewhere partying. Tonight, however, there was a light under her door, which Kid knew meant she had a visitor and wasn't to be disturbed. Not that Kid would want to disturb her. Nadine always had a short fuse, particularly when she'd been out drinking. Besides, Kid had better things to do.

He looked around. The box he'd come rushing home to open wasn't anywhere obvious. He checked the hall. Checked the kitchen. Checked the sitting room, under the table and behind the sofa where his bedding was kept. Ever since the message had come down the long, convoluted line of his mother's friends and acquaintances that, when she'd died, she'd left behind a box with his name on it, Kid had been trying to retrieve it. He'd gone round every last person he could think of, trying to find out where it was, but it had got him nowhere – until tonight.

Kid found the box at last – in the bath. One flap had been torn, as if somebody like Nadine had tried to see inside. The other had his name on it – the one he never used, printed in full beneath the name he was known by. Marcus Aurelius Cato. His real name.

Kid stood for ages, staring down at the box. All evening he'd been imagining what might be inside, but now just having it in front of him felt like enough. Opening it wasn't necessary. In fact, opening it was only going to make his mother seem more dead than she already was, because then everything about her would be in the past.

But then everything about her already *was* in the past, Kid told himself, and it had been for a long time. Kid closed his eyes, trying to track back in his memory past the sometimes frightening, sometimes endearing, strange, batty, unpredictable person his mother had become to the person she'd been when he was small. His memories were a warren of hidden byways and things he'd rather forget, but the ones he wanted to remember were all lost.

'This is stupid,' Kid said at last. 'Just get on with it.'

He climbed into the bath and started ripping open the box. On top, wrapped in tissue paper as if it was fine porcelain, he found an old tin kettle which had a hole in the bottom and wasn't even the plug-in sort. He put it on one side and lifted out another tissue-paper offering which turned out to be a squashed hat. He bashed it into shape. It was made of red, yellow and emerald-green feathers and resembled a flower-pot.

Kid hung it over the taps, unable to imagine his mother wearing any sort of hat, let alone this one. Then he dived back into the box and pulled out a pair of baby dungarees worn through at the knees, a steam iron burned out at the plug and an old toaster which smelt like the grills at work when they hadn't been cleaned.

Kid shook the crumbs out into the toilet, then

stuck it on the floor underneath the basin. The cardboard box was half empty by now, but so far he'd found nothing to get excited about. What he'd been hoping for were personal things – old photographs, letters, maybe even diaries which might unlock the mystery of who his mother really was and what had made her the person she became. He dived down again, pulling out a bag of tangled Christmas fairylights, a plastic angel and a box of brightly coloured glass baubles that he vaguely recognised from Christmases long ago when the two of them had had a proper home.

Kid threw the whole lot on the floor, then brought up a pair of ladies pyjamas and a thin cotton dressing-gown, a towel, some slippers, a crumpled dress which he recognised, a couple of blank postcards from exotic places and a wallet which had no money in it, but did at least contain a photograph of him.

Kid pocketed the wallet, but threw aside the rest. Then he dug down into the box one final time, coming up with his birth certificate and two envelopes, on one of which had been written the word MOTHER – which Kid guessed meant the grandmother he'd never met – and the other, on which was written the word KID.

That had been the only name Kid's mother had

ever used for him. His other, longer name had always been unspoken. It had been *Kid, come here*, or *You there, Kid*, or *Hey, Kid*, or, as now, just plain *Kid* on its own.

Kid climbed out of the bath. The box was empty now, but this was what he'd been looking for. Back in the sitting room he made up the sofa bed and climbed into it, then sat staring at the envelope as if afraid of opening it. Finally he slit it open and shook out a collection of pages covered in his mother's handwriting, which went in every direction, ignoring all the lines. Kid spread out the pages on the bedcover, and sat before them. Every inch of paper was covered. There was scarcely any space between the lines. It was as if Kid's mother had been trying to cram in everything she wanted to say before running out of pen or paper or time, but the result was that it was all completely unintelligible.

All the same, Kid read it through, trying to make sense of it. But his mother had never made much sense and in this, her last letter, nothing had changed there. Only at the bottom of the last page was anything legible, Kid's mother abandoning her scrawl to print her words carefully.

'It's not very pretty,' she'd written. 'But there you are. He was a devil, that man. A charmer, but a devil too. I never wanted you to grow up like him. Never even wanted you to know he existed, let alone was your father and me his wife. God help me. What was I ever thinking of? I'm sorry Kid.'

A wife. Kid's mother had once been somebody's wife. Kid shook out the envelope again, hoping for another page to give him an explanation. There was no other page, but a photograph fell out of a black man with a flower in his button-hole, and a white woman who was a dead ringer for the mother Kid had been trying to remember earlier. The man was dressed in a pin-striped suit. The woman wore the feathered hat. It really didn't suit her but she wore it with pride. She wasn't dressed in white, but she too had a flower in her lapel and it was obviously her wedding day.

Kid stared at the photograph, taking in the man's features, realising with a shock that he looked just like an older version of himself. He'd always known he must have a father somewhere, but it had never crossed his mind that his mother had married him and that Cato might be his father's name as well as his.

Kid picked up the hat that, even all these years later, his mother had kept. Then he turned to his birth certificate, registered in the District of Wandsworth, and read it line by line. His mother's middle name was Edith, which Kid had never known, and his father's name was Marcus Aurelius Cato, just like his own. His occupation was recorded as 'businessman', which came as a surprise to Kid because he couldn't imagine someone as other-worldly as his mother marrying some fancy, big-deal businessman.

But it was Kid's father's place of residence that came as the bigger surprise. Belize City, said the certificate. And where the hell was that? Kid knew where Brixton was, and Battersea, Brockwell Park and Balham. But up until that moment he'd never heard of Belize.

2

A Little Country on the Caribbean Coast

It took time, but Kid tracked it down. He wasn't much of a one for geography, but he knew how to use the internet. In the end, having expected to find Belize first in Africa, then Asia, he finally found it on the Caribbean coast, part of the thin cluster of nations keeping North and South America apart.

Zooming in on Google Earth, Kid looked down upon a strip of coastline covered with jungle. Occasionally the canopy of trees was intersected by sandy tracks or the line of a river, and occasionally a handful of villages emerged, or even a town. One of them, right on the coast, had to be the capital, Kid reckoned. But west, south and north of it, there was nothing but jungle except for the occasional green-clad mountain.

What sort of businessman, Kid wondered, hailed from a country like this? How had his mother met him, and where was he right now? Kid re-read his mother's letter, trying to find out more, but with no success. Then he scoured the photograph, but he couldn't even figure out where it was taken, England or Belize.

After that, however, Kid was obsessed with Belize. This was his exam year and his school work was piling up, but finding out about his father's homeland seemed far more important. He'd stare at the postcards which were all of Belize, and wonder how they'd come into his mother's hands. Had she been there? Had she even married there? And what was Belize like? Far more than toasters and burned-out kettles, it felt like Kid's real inheritance.

Again and again, he returned to the internet, a picture growing in his mind of a lush, green country with white sand beaches and clear turquoise seas. A picture grew as well of a successful, wealthy businessman-father, living in a big white house with not only servants, lawns and a pool, but a family too. Out there in Belize could be half-brothers and sisters, grandparents, aunties and uncles who, if Kid could only find them, would welcome him with open arms.

One day, Kid thought, I'll go out there and find out what it's like for myself. Then he thought, I'll go when my exams are over. Then, why wait? Once I've saved the money, I'll just go.

After this, Kid spent every available spare minute doing extra shifts at Jet's. His teachers nagged him because he was always off school, but he couldn't have cared less. Sometimes he started at Jet's at eleven in the morning and crawled into bed after midnight. The savings were growing, but the cost of the trip was growing too. It wasn't only an air fare that Kid had to save for. It was his living expenses once he'd arrived in Belize – buses, food and hostels. He already had a passport, thanks to a booze cruise he'd once been on with his mother and some of her friends, so he didn't have to pay for that. But he did have to pay to be inoculated against all the terrible diseases that he read about on the internet – malaria, rabies and things like that.

Nadine thought the whole thing was a joke at first. It took her a while to realise that Kid was serious. When he started lecturing her like a professor on Belize's geography or history, its mixture of different languages and religions and its racial types, she thought he'd flipped. So what if Mestizos spoke Spanish and had Indian blood, and Creoles were Afro-Europeans who spoke a form of English known as Kriol? What did it matter if the Garifuna people were descended from shipwrecked Africans who'd escaped their fate as slaves? Or that the Kekchi and Mopan Mayans were descended from a race of temple-builders who had all died out?

It mattered to Kid, though. He'd go from his father's photograph to the mirror and back again, looking for clues in his skin-colour, cheek-bone structure, jaw line, nose, lips, eyes and hair. Was he Garifuna? No, he wasn't black enough. Or Mestizo? No, he was too black.

While Kid agonised, Nadine acquired a new boyfriend who virtually moved in. His name was Kyle and before long the flat was full of his things. Suddenly it felt like a cupboard and looked like one too. Kyle had so much clobber that it was hard to get across the room. Even opening out the sofa bed became a problem, what with Kyle and Nadine lounging all over it, watching telly and making love.

Finally, Nadine had a little word. Romance was in the air and Kid was in the way. 'Here,' she said, thrusting wads of money at him. 'This is for you. Find a room of your own. Or, if you're really serious about it, blow the whole lot on getting out to Belize. I don't care, but you've got to go. I'm really sorry, but we need the space.'

Kid stared at the money and didn't know what to say. It was more than he'd saved even doing extra shifts. In fact, he'd never seen so much money in his life.

'Cheers,' he said. 'Seeing as you don't want me,

perhaps that's what I'll do. I'll pay you back of course, so don't you worry about that.'

Nadine blushed. At least she had the grace to do that. It wasn't that she didn't want him, she said, and she didn't need paying back. She was only trying to help. Kyle too. He'd chipped in as well. He was a good bloke. He'd give his last penny to help someone out.

The next day, Kid took the day off school and booked his flight instead – one way only because he'd no intention of ever coming back, no matter what Nadine had said. A sense of unreality hung over him. Only later in the day, bumping into Jaydene Lewis from his class at school, did Kid realise what he'd done.

'I've done it all myself, flight, hotel, the whole thing,' he said. 'I'm off in a couple of days and I'm never coming back.'

Jaydene looked shocked. Posho Jaydene Lewis, with the wealthy parents who did everything for her, and the big house.

'You're doing *what?*' she said. 'What about your exams? And you can't just go, anyway. You need visas and things like that.'

Kid said he could do anything he wanted, and nobody could stop him. He was free, he said, unlike her. That shut her up.

Kid went home and told Kyle what he'd done. Nadine was nowhere to be seen. Kyle looked deeply uncomfortable. 'Are you sure you know what you're doing?' he said.

'I've never been surer,' Kid said.

There was one last thing that Kid had to do, except for pack. That night he rode out to Richmond on the underground and tracked down his unknown grandmother's address.

The house looked very grand, with a lawn in the front garden and steps up to the front door. Kid stood looking up at it. All he knew about the woman inside was that she'd thrown his mother out for hanging about with a wild crowd, drinking too much and having a baby – who'd been him, of course.

For a long time, Kid stood across the road, looking up at the windows. He knew he wanted to ring the bell but in the end he simply stuffed the envelope through the letter box instead and turned and fled.

3

A ONE-WAY TICKET

After that Kid was shocked by the speed at which things happened. All next day he was plunged into a frenzy of last-minute preparations. There were possessions to be given away, because no way was Kid taking everything with him, and then there was shopping to be done, including everything from malaria pills to a rucksack. Kid spent a long time trying to pack his rucksack, forcing everything in, and then rushed off to Jet's for a final shift that he was determined no one would forget.

It was traditional at Jet's for food fights to take place when anybody left. Eggs would be pelted, bombs made out of bags of mayonnaise, and water-pistols fired with ketchup and tartar sauce. This time, however, Kid wanted to do something a bit different. Whilst everybody's back was turned, he sneaked round the kitchen setting all the burger timers for eleven o'clock, then screwing them all away behind the grills where no one would be able to reach them to switch off.

Sure enough, next morning at eleven, Kid received a call from Jet. The timers were all screaming and nobody could get to them because the grills were at their hottest at eleven o'clock.

'You've lost me all my bloody customers,' Jet yelled. 'You're finished in the burger business. Don't think I'll ever have you back!'

Kid knew that Jet didn't mean it. He was still laughing about it all when Kyle appeared, to drive him to the airport. As he'd been expecting to make his way there on public transport, this came as a surprise. So, too, did the present that Kyle held out to him.

'Here,' he said. 'These are for you.'

Kid took possession of a pair of thick-soled army boots which, by a happy coincidence, happened to fit. 'Cheers,' he said, throwing away his aged trainers with worn soles.

'You're welcome,' Kyle replied.

Downstairs – also to Kid's surprise – he found Nadine waiting in Kyle's car, ready for the airport too and looking decidedly guilty.

'All this stuff you've been saying about not coming back,' she said, 'you don't mean it, do you? You do know that you can stay with us again. Any time you're stuck. You've only got to ask.'

'Just don't stay too long, hey?' Kid said.

Nadine flushed. 'Actually, I've enjoyed your company,' she said, which Kid took as some kind of victory.

At the airport, Kid found everybody going places and in a rush. He was surrounded by backpackers, business people huddled over laptops, families making fond farewells, old people struggling with luggage, children dashing about and air hostesses in crisp uniforms heading purposefully down the great hall, looking as if they were the only ones who knew what was going on.

Feeling nervous and agitated, Kid attempted to run his passport through the automatic check-in machine but it kept on being spat out. After three attempts, a voice behind him said, 'You've got the thing the wrong way round.' Kid turned about to find a straggly, blonde-haired girl behind him, with startlingly green eyes and a rucksack just like his.

'Here,' she said. 'This is what you do . . .'

Like an old hand, she took Kid's passport, turned it round and shoved it back into the machine. Immediately everything started working properly.

'Thanks,' Kid said, thinking that if he couldn't even get this right, what hope was there for him alone in Belize?

'No problem,' the girl replied.

Later, Kid saw her again. By this time, he'd said goodbye to Kyle and Nadine and gone through security where his hand luggage had bleeped and he'd had to empty out its entire contents, including his mother's hat, which had caused a few wry smiles. Now he was mooching round the duty-free shops, and the girl caught his attention, buying magazines and chocolate. She looked up, saw him watching her, smiled and walked away to join a group of friends.

Everybody else, it seemed, had friends to talk to, if not in person at least on the phone. Only Kid was all alone. He bought himself a Coke and waited for his plane to be called. It was the first time for days now that he'd sat down without something that needed to be done.

A couple sat next to him – an old man and his son. The old man was flying out to Hong Kong, where he'd once lived.

'It was fifty years ago to this very day,' he said, 'that I sailed out. Sailed, mark you, not flew. And do you know how I chose it as my destination? I opened the map, and there were all the countries coloured in British Empire red and I thought which shall I choose, because all of them were mine. My inheritance, don't you know. My birthright. Well, I went to Hong Kong and that's where I met your mother. And the rest is history.'

It sure was, Kid thought. The British Empire – what was that about? When Kid's gate was called, he found a group of backpackers ready to board, all reminding him of Jaydene Lewis and her noisy, show-off group of friends. His heart sank at the thought of being stuck with rich, spoilt types like these, but amongst them all he saw the blonde-haired girl who'd helped him with his passport. And, though he didn't want to admit it, it was good to feel that someone on the plane wasn't a total stranger.

Kid walked through the gate as if ordinary life had been left behind. His sense of standing on the edge of the unknown was overwhelming. He tried to imagine Belize waiting to greet him at the end of his journey, but all he could conjure up was blank-ness. Everything he'd read about the country was lost to him.

What am I doing? Kid asked himself. This is crazy. What does Belize mean to me? I hadn't even heard of it until a few months ago. And as for my father – he probably doesn't even live there any more. And, even if he does, how am I going to find him? I haven't worked out a plan or anything.

Kid was on the plane by now, being greeted by

the cabin crew. It was the first time he'd ever flown, and every instinct in him said to turn and run. But he walked down the aisle instead, checking the numbers and then stowing his hand luggage. His seat was right next to the window, and Kid sat and buckled up. The screen in front of him flickered into life, explaining important safety information, but he closed his eyes. He didn't want to know about emergencies. Things like that were too scary to think about.

The cabin crew came down the aisles closing all the overhead compartments. Everybody was seated now and the jet's massive engines had started to throb. Either this had to be the worst day of his life, Kid decided, or it was the best. But he didn't know which.

The plane eased out of its berth and started taxiing. A strange calmness descended upon Kid. It was too late to turn back, wasn't it? He looked through the window at the distant airport perimeter. Suddenly the moment he'd been planning for all this time had arrived. It was right here. Right now. *It was happening*.

The plane let out a furious roar, then started down the runway, hurtling ever faster, pinning Kid back in his seat. And this *was* the best day of his life, no matter how nervous he felt. Here he was, taking a risk, seizing his chance. No way could it be anything else.

Suddenly, in the single most beautiful moment of Kid's life, the plane rose into the air. For an instant he caught a glimpse of airport buildings and of other planes behind theirs, queuing up for take-off, their tails gleaming like sharks' fins in the wintry light. Then they were gone, and the airport was gone too. And then London was gone, because the grid of roads beneath him didn't look like anywhere Kid recognised. And then the only world he had ever known was gone too.

He let out his breath. Up here in the sky, the air was golden. But the land beneath him lay wintry and dark. It was yesterday's land and it belonged to the past. Yet here there was no past, or future either for that matter. Only a sun setting somewhere on the edge of the sky, and a plane chased after it, holding back time.

4

WELCOME TO BELIZE

That sense of time being held back lasted for all seven hours of the flight across the Atlantic. Even after Kid had watched an entire movie on the screen in front of him, nothing much had changed – the sun, still evident in the sky, seemingly unwilling to set. Kid watched it through the window, reduced to a thin strip of red. He was determined to witness the moment when it finally disappeared. But, in the end, it beat him because he fell asleep.

Kid awoke later to find that darkness had fallen and the cabin crew were bringing round a meal. Unexpectedly hungry, he ate everything in front of him. There was something comforting about aeroplane food. It certainly didn't look much, stuck inside its cellophane wrappers, but when he'd finished eating, Kid felt surprisingly full.

He watched another film after that. Then he listened

to some music and tried to relax. The flight continued smoothly, cutting through the darkness with no end in sight. Even the rowdy backpackers were silenced by the length of the flight. Kid peered all around him. Across a sea of faces he could see the blonde girl looking bored. He willed her to glance his way. Her smile would have broken up the monotony. But it never happened.

Kid slept again until awoken by the pilot's announcement that they were making their descent. The cabin crew came down the aisles, handing out landing passes and customs declarations along with dire warnings of what the US authorities might do if they weren't completed properly.

Kid filled in his details, agonising over whether his handwriting was clear and his spelling correct. What would happen if he'd got something wrong? Would he be arrested? Kid had never met an American before. All he knew was what he'd seen on the telly – a nation of fast-talking men and women who carried guns and didn't stand for shit.

An hour later, however, leaving the US Immigration area with his face scrutinised, his fingerprints recorded and his passport in his hand, Kid was a free man. A massive neon sign welcomed him to JOHN F. KENNEDY, NEW YORK but the enormous arrivals hall where he now stood looked remarkably similar to the airport he'd left seven hours before.

Kid looked round for somewhere to make himself comfortable until his connecting flight early next morning. It was midnight now. All the bars and restaurants had closed and the best seats for sleeping on had been grabbed by hardened travellers who knew the score. He found a bit of floor and curled up, keeping his belongings close for fear of being robbed. The hall was broken into sound zones. At one end he could hear a cleaning machine whirring as it picked up litter and polished the floor. Then, closer, he could hear the clack of a coffee machine. Then, closer still, he could hear the snoring of fellow travellers.

Kid wriggled on the floor, sleeping sometimes but sometimes wide awake, thinking not only about the long journey that had brought him here, but the one that had started years before this flight. He thought about his mother and all the places they had lived. There had been times when things had been steady for a while, with proper cooked meals and the two of them watching telly together and sometimes even sharing the same bed, as if he was still a baby.

But things had always gone wrong. There had always been some freak-out with his mother losing her rag and whoever they were living with wanting them out. Every time she'd sworn it wouldn't happen again, but in the end it had been Kid who'd said *never again*. His mother could do her thing, and he'd do his. She could look after herself and he'd look after Number One.

Kid awoke at regular intervals to check the clock, but he still managed to oversleep and nearly miss his connecting flight. In a panic he dashed for the gate and was the last person to board the plane. By the time he'd woken up properly, New York was a thing of the past and so was the winter.

Kid shivered with excitement. Summertime lay ahead of him now and so did Belize. Even so, it took several more hours, flying over the strange wilderness of the Florida Everglades, before he finally sensed the world beneath him really changing. Khaki-coloured mud flats lay beneath him, and weird turquoise lagoons. The sun shone on them, making them sparkle like baked enamel.

Kid drifted off to sleep, waking once or twice to see what his neighbour said was the Gulf of Mexico glistening beneath him. Finally he awoke to find that the sea had disappeared and miles of jungle lay beneath him, stretching away to the horizon like a green tufted carpet. Occasionally a sandy track broke it up, then disappeared. In the distance Kid could see a mountain range. Once he glimpsed an empty road running straight as an arrow with not a car in sight.

It took Kid a while to realise that this had to be Belize. Even though he'd seen the jungle on Google Earth, nothing had prepared him for how big it was, rolling on for what looked like ever. Only when the pilot announced that Belize City was approaching, and they were making their descent, did he really grasp that he'd arrived.

Kid saw a green river breaking out of the jungle, then beyond it the first real sign of habitation in the form of electricity pylons, a network of small roads and a smattering of tiny, matchstick buildings. The plane banked steeply and Kid looked down, unable to tear his eyes away. After such a long journey, everything was suddenly happening so quickly. There was the river again, flowing into the sea, and there the city centre and there, beyond the trees on the rim of the city, the airport.

In fact, *here* was the airport, not *there,* and the undercarriage was engaging with it, and the plane was tearing along the runway and finally juddering to a halt. And this was it at last, Belize at last. *Kid had arrived.*

Grabbing his hand luggage, Kid was amongst the first down the aisle, stepping out into a wall of heat that slapped him in the face like a hot wet towel. Kid had known that a tropical region like this was bound to be hot, but nothing had prepared him for how hot heat could be. He staggered down the steps to an airport concourse that sizzled like the fryers at Jet's. Reaching the shade of the terminal building came as a relief.

Kid queued in a blissfully air-conditioned hall to hand in his landing papers, shuffling forwards slowly, in no hurry to return outside. Ahead of him he could see the Belizean flag with two men on it, one black, one white, sheltering in the shade of a huge green tree. They'd need it, he reckoned, if the weather outside was typical.

Kid handed in his papers and showed his passport, then collected his rucksack from the baggage recovery point and finally headed for the door at the end of the hall. He could sense the heat beyond it waiting to pounce. But something else was out there, waiting too.

Kid had noticed it the minute he'd got off the plane. A smell had hit him that he couldn't find words for because 'earthy', 'wet' or 'spicy' wouldn't have been quite right. And, caught up with the smell, Kid had heard a voice.

It was as if the two things were sides of the same coin, the smell and the voice. And now, as the doors slid back to allow Kid through, he heard it again. The smell was of trees, and the voice was theirs as well, whispering, *'Welcome to Belize.'*

PART TWO

BELIZE

5

BAD STREETS

As Kid stood squinting in the sun, a press of people rushed to greet him claiming to be taxi drivers and trying to get his luggage off him. He knew from life back home never to trust strangers, not even smiling ones with offers of help. But here, blinking in the sunlight of a strange country, he found his rucksack being taken off him before he could stop it happening, and bundled into a battered-looking car. Then he was bundled in too and, before he'd got his bearings, the car was pulling away from the curb.

'Where yu goin'?' his driver asked.

Kid hoped he hadn't been picked up by some crook who'd charge him a small fortune and dump him if he couldn't pay. He was booked into the Ocean Hotel, he said. Had the driver heard of it?

The taxi driver nodded. 'Dat's a good place, maan, good cheap, good sounds, good food,' he said, tearing out of the airport complex, music blaring from his speakers.

Kid tried to relax. The sun was shining, so why not, the windows were down and the driver seemed genuinely friendly. Not only that, but the music he was playing couldn't have suited its surroundings better. It was dusty music, sun-shining music, the music of dirt roads and sizzling heat.

The driver sang along, stopping occasionally to ask Kid questions. Where did he come from, England or the US? And how long was he staying?

Kid said he didn't know. The driver said that was the best way. 'See how tings go,' he said, speaking what Kid realised had to be the Kriol language he'd read about on the internet. 'Keep yu opshaans open, stay loose. Dat's de way we do tings in Beleez.'

By now, the taxi was following the path of a river, the sunlight sparkling on its surface making it look a luscious emerald green. It wasn't the only car on the road, but it tore along as if it was. At the city limits, a row of clapboard houses came into view, with shuttered windows and built on stilts. The taxi passed a couple of factories, followed by a cement works, and the streets began to narrow. Suddenly they were hemmed in by massive logging trucks and dusty four-by-fours with smoke-grey windows and huge chrome fenders.

The taxi slowed down for the only set of traffic lights Kid would ever see in Belize, but didn't stop completely. Kid just had time to see the 'Jesus Lover of My Soul' Baptist Church before the driver jumped the lights, and then he saw the 'Jesus Lover of My Soul' school beyond it, followed by a cinderblock supermarket and a nightclub with chains on all the doors and windows, and men sitting out front as if waiting for it to open.

Shops and bars were pressing in on either side now, but Kid told himself this couldn't possibly be the centre of Belize City – not with broken sidewalks, pot-holed roads, stinking ditches and stray dogs wandering about. The sidewalks were crowded with people, mostly black- or copper-skinned, but Kid saw the occasional white skin too, and even glimpsed some pink as well, denoting tourists in the area.

The taxi made its way over what the driver called the 'swing-bridge', but even when they reached the commercial district on the other side, with its hotels, banks and shops, Kid had no idea that this was the city centre. The shops were too shabby, and the sidewalks too cluttered with vendors, their merchandise spread out around them. One stick-thin man stared into space as if he didn't know where he was. Another had a few wares around him – packets of tea, a plastic doll, a pile of silver tinsel, a sliced white loaf.

The taxi turned a corner, just past this last man, and an empty alley stretched ahead of them. Kid stiffened like a dog sensing danger. Where was the driver taking him? There were no hotels down this alley, nor were there any people. What was wrong with sticking to the main road?

At the end of the alley, the driver turned again, and Kid found himself on the waterfront, caught between a suspiciously brown-looking sea and a run-down clapboard building with wonky-looking wooden steps and iron grilles at all its windows. The road was cracked and full of weeds. This certainly didn't look like a tourist spot. For a terrible moment, Kid thought he'd been kidnapped.

Only when the driver said, 'Dis is it – de Oshaan Hotel,' did it dawn on Kid that he'd reached his destination. He tumbled out of the car, trying to hide the fact that he'd been scared. The driver dragged his rucksack out of the boot. Kid paid the fare, relief washing over him. But only after the driver had gone did he realise he'd paid twice the going rate by using US dollars instead of Belizean ones.

What did money count for though, compared to arriving alive and in one piece? Kid climbed up the hotel steps and opened a creaking wooden door.

The Ocean Hotel didn't look anything like its picture on the internet. Inside, instead of potted palms and colonial charm, he found a dusty reception desk and a sleeping receptionist who only stirred himself for long enough to sign him in, check his passport, and hand him his key, but whose duties didn't extend to showing him where to go.

Kid found his room eventually, despite the number having dropped off the door. It was on the second floor, set back behind a wide communal balcony and bathed in the sorts of smells only to be expected from an ocean that was brown. The room was basic, but Kid reckoned it had everything he needed – a bed, a chair, a fan, a cupboard and a shower room and toilet. When Kid switched on the shower, though, instead of water a couple of geckos came tumbling out. Then, when he switched on the electric fan, nothing happened and when he lay on the bed, the mattress was so soft that he almost disappeared into it. No wonder the room was cheap, Kid thought. But too tired to care, he rolled over in the bed and fell asleep. It was as if he was a light and he'd been switched off.

A couple of hours later, Kid awoke to a din outside the hotel. It was so loud that he jumped out of bed. What was going on? Hearing whistles, trumpets, drums, shouting voices and even snatches of singing, he went and leant over the balcony. A group of young people dressed in red-and-white shirts were coming along the waterfront bearing banners announcing 'VOTE UDP' and 'IT'S TIME FOR CHANGE'. When they saw Kid watching them, they waved and shouted up to him and he waved back. Change was fine by him, he reckoned. It was what he'd come here for.

The procession carried on past the hotel, only to meet another one coming the other way, this time dressed in blue and white. Each procession carried banners showing different men, but their warnings about what would happen to Belize if their party didn't get in, were remarkably similar.

Kid left them to it, shouting at each other and waving their banners. He thought about going back to sleep, but hadn't eaten since last night so decided to look for the hotel dining room instead. This, to his disappointment, had closed down two years ago, but the local supermarket was only two blocks away according to the reception boy and anything he bought could be eaten in his room.

Out in the hot sun, and with what felt like the whole of Belize City watching him, Kid took a while to get his bearings. When he finally found the super-market, however, he discovered an Aladdin's cave selling everything from baked beans to massive knives with big handles, called machetes. He could have bought mangoes, guavas or fresh papaya if he'd wanted, but opted for what he knew best and bought a day's supply of Snickers bars and a couple of Coca-Colas instead.

At the till, fumbling with a wallet full of unfamiliar notes and coins, again Kid felt as if everybody was staring at him.

'Heah. Give it heah. Ai tek it fi you,' the till-girl said.

Feeling small, foreign and completely helpless, Kid allowed the girl to raid his wallet, then slunk away, sure he'd been short-changed but too afraid to complain. It was a relief to return to the Ocean Hotel and get away from all those prying eyes.

Kid sat on the balcony, stuffing down Snickers bars one after another. Waves broke over the sea wall and great prehistoric-looking birds made circles in the sky above the hotel. Boys went by on bikes, dodging pot-holes and larking about. Then a group of girls went by as well, dressed in white uniforms with bright red buttons. Where were they going? Was it the end of their school day? Kid knew nothing about Belize City, for all his exploring on the internet. The reality was different to anything he'd read about.

Kid shivered with excitement. By now the

Snickers bars had done the trick and he felt ready to face the unknown. Locking his room, he headed off again, passing the supermarket and all the banks, crossing the swing-bridge and making his way along a shopping street which seemed to sell everything from wedding dresses to fresh fish.

When Kid had passed the last shop on this street, he crossed the road and started down a smaller one which appeared to loop back towards the bridge. Before he'd gone very far, however, a man in a red vest approached. 'Wha fi yu gaan down heah?' he said. 'Heah's a bad street. Bad pipple live heah. Yu wan go dat weh . . .'

The man pointed with a bony finger, back the way Kid had come, saying that Queen Street was a nice one where he'd find fellow tourists and nice shops. Kid thanked the man and headed back, but the man came after him, his eyes on Kid's pocket where he plainly kept his wallet, reckoning his advice was worth paying for.

Kid kept his wallet where it was. Not for nothing had he grown up on the streets of south London. When he reached Queen Street again all the shops were closed. Suddenly it was sundown. Night was falling faster than Kid had expected, and street lighting, he discovered, wasn't one of Belize City's better features.

As Kid hurried back towards the swing-bridge, a new companion suddenly appeared. Like a shadow, he stuck to Kid's side – a tall, thin man with dreadlocks and a smile.

'Ai George de Jamaican. Weh yu from, maan? England? Well, it's good to meet yu. Let mi shake yu by de hand. Yu English, wi love yu heah. Yu like mi recite yu a poem? Yu like a song?'

Kid didn't want either, but he got both. All the way back over the swing-bridge to the hotel, George the Jamaican sang to him, complimented him and recited poetry for which he claimed he wanted a dollar. Only a dollar, he said, but Kid refused to give him anything. All George wanted, he knew, was for Kid to get out his wallet.

Finally, as Kid had been dreading, George turned nasty. 'Wai yu be so mean?' he snapped. 'Ai pay yu compliment. Ai recite poem an' sing yu song. And what yu give me fi return? What's a dollar to yu fockin' English pipple? Yu bleedin' us poor Bileezans dry.'

'I thought you were Jamaican,' Kid said.

This was a mistake. George the Jamaican put his hand to his chest as if he had a knife in there somewhere, and repeated his demand. Kid started walking faster, but couldn't shake him off.

'I didn't ask for your compliment,' he said. 'That

43

was your choice. I didn't ask for a song or a poem.'

'Den yu shoulda tol' mi to piss off.'

By now Kid could see the Ocean Hotel ahead. He hurried faster, telling himself he'd only got a few more steps. 'Why should I do that?' he said as he reached the steps and headed up them. 'I came all this way to meet Belizean people, not tell them to piss off.'

Kid rushed through the hotel door and felt it slam behind him, praying that George wouldn't come after him. For a moment his assailant stood outside growling like a bear. But then he turned and walked away, and it was left to the boy behind the reception desk to say – as if Kid didn't know that now already – 'Wha fi yu go out after dark? Bileez City isn' a safe place.'

6

'DA BOY LOOKIN' FI HE DADDY'

Back in his room Kid tried to relax with a nice, long shower but there still wasn't any water so he flung himself on to the bed instead and tried to sleep. What else was there to do? He didn't have a telly. He didn't know a soul. He was fresh from England, and had no proper plan. And, besides, his long day had exhausted him.

Unfortunately for Kid, however, an election meeting had just started down the street, and he could hear every word. Apparently the country was in mortal danger if there was no change in government. But was it really necessary to shout about it? And did it take quite so many different people to repeat the same things?

Kid finally fell asleep, but awoke in the early hours of the morning to find that he'd left his mosquito screen open and was covered in bites. But at

45

least the election meeting was over, he told himself, and the worst he had to listen to now was a little breeze blowing in off the sea, and the rustling of palms along the waterfront.

Kid awoke next at dawn to find that the breeze had turned into a heady wind which sent cans rattling down the street. He lay listening to them, wondering what the new day would bring and feeling his first real twinge of serious apprehension. What exactly was he meant to do now that he was here? Kid had imagined himself wandering about Belize, acquainting himself with the country and feeling in his bones that he'd come home. Tracking down his father had always come afterwards.

But listening to Belize City awakening around him, and realising that he didn't know a soul, suddenly all Kid wanted to do was find his father. Behind everything he'd told himself he'd come here for, this was it. It didn't matter whether his father was rich or not, or had a family or not. Just knowing another person in this strange, lonely country would be enough.

Kid went down to the reception desk to borrow a phone book. His father could live right here in Belize City, he told himself. He could get up every day within striking distance of this hotel, and pass it every morning on his way to work. By some chance of fate he could be passing it even now.

Back in his bedroom, Kid started going through the book, only to find that it was divided up by districts, which meant it was necessary to know where a person lived before looking for their number. Not only that, but most numbers were businesses and the rest were cell-phone that didn't come with addresses.

Kid had guessed that finding his father would be a long shot, but he hadn't expected even the phone book to be against him. He read the whole thing from cover to cover, but found no Catos. Worse still, this wasn't just the directory for Belize City. It covered the entire country.

Later, when Kid returned the directory to the reception desk, he found a woman in charge, not the boy. Not that she was any friendlier, glaring at the book as if Kid had stolen it.

'I was looking for a man called Marcus Aurelius Cato,' Kid said. 'You don't know him, do you?' He guessed it wasn't likely, but at least it was worth a try.

The woman shook her head. Even when Kid returned to his room and came back with his father's photograph, she still shook her head. Why didn't he take it round town? she said. Maybe someone else would recognise it.

Reckoning this was a good idea, Kid set off for the

supermarket. Maybe the woman behind the till would know something, or the school kids on their bikes, or some electioneering member of either the UDP or the PUP. Maybe a taxi driver might know, or the teller in one of the banks, or even a policeman on the street.

It was a long shot, Kid knew, but in this country where he didn't know a soul what other leads had he got?

Kid asked all morning, but with no luck. He didn't ask some people because they looked too dodgy, but he approached anyone who looked as if they'd give him a straight answer. Not that it got him anywhere. Neither in the supermarket, nor the bank next door, nor the music shop on the corner with massive speakers stacked in the doorway, nor on the street, nor even squatting on the sidewalks with their wares around them, had anyone seen the man in the photograph or heard his name.

Kid asked all over the city centre, but with no more luck. He asked at the water terminal, where boats went in and out to the cayes, taking tourists on diving holidays. He asked at the bus station. Asked in the offices of shipping and logging companies, but always with the same answer.

Finally Kid started fanning out across the city, asking even dodgy people, not caring if they wanted a dollar for their answer. Soon he found himself lost in a network of streets that looked increasingly rundown. He stood at a crossroads, not knowing which road to take. Children circled him on battered-looking bikes, and women looked down at him from balconies as if silently questioning what he, a stranger, was doing in their midst.

Kid decided to turn back. But which way was back? Every street looked alike. Which way was the city centre? Kid was so hot and tired that he couldn't work it out. In fact he was so hot that he could scarcely think at all. Sweat rolled down his neck, armpits and chest. It rolled down his brows into his eyes.

'Yu wan' a drink?' a voice called out.

Kid looked up. On the opposite corner of the crossroad stood a house almost buried in rambling bougainvillea, a scrawny-looking Creole woman standing on its balcony, her hair in yellow curlers.

'You bet,' Kid said. 'I'd give anything for a drink.' And he meant it.

'Then yu better come up an' get one.'

Kid didn't need to be told twice. He crossed the road and leapt up the woman's steps to receive a plastic cup of crushed pineapple and ice, and a lecture on venturing out on bad streets like these, where it wasn't safe for strangers to walk. Kid explained that he was looking for someone, and showed the woman his photograph. He didn't need to tell her that the man in it was his father. At just one glance, the woman could see that. The world was full of children looking for their daddies, she said, and daddies trying not to be found. But the real daddy – the Lor Jeezas Krise, who was the daddy of them all – he was the one Kid should be looking for, not this man here.

Kid stared at the woman blankly.

'Mek yu love da Lor' Jeezas Krise?' the woman said.

'Do I what?' Kid said.

'God bring yu back to life with Jeezas Krise,' the woman said, warming to her subject. 'Da son a God – yu ever heah a him?'

Kid had heard of the Son of God. He'd also heard of scary sects where people grabbed you off the streets and did weird things to your brain. Draining his pineapple drink, he bid the woman a hasty farewell. No, he didn't want to hear her witnessing tonight at the Church of the Glorious Sisterhood, he called as headed off down the street.

Belize City was a dangerous place. Even the people who seemed nice and kindly seemed to want something out of you. Kid broke into a steady trot. Gradually the streets became familiar and he realised that he was back in the city centre again.

Better still, he was close to the hotel which, just at that moment, felt like the only safe place.

Why had he come here? Kid asked himself. He must have been crazy, buying a one-way ticket. What was he going to do with himself now that he was here? Was everywhere in the country as threatening and downright scary as Belize City?

The sleepy reception boy was back on duty when Kid came through the door. But he dragged his eyes open as Kid went past, and announced that a note had been left for him.

Kid took an envelope which had obviously been opened, which meant the boy knew what it said. Printed carefully on it, underlined twice, were the words *TO DA BOY LOOKIN' FI HE DADDY.*

'Who gave you this?' Kid said.

The boy shrugged. 'Nobody,' he said. 'I jus' look up, an' dere it was.'

Kid waited until he was back in his room before tearing open the envelope. Inside he found a single sheet of paper folded over several times. He smoothed it out and read:

'EVERYTING HE TOUCH TURN TO SAND, BUT HE NOT BAD AS PIPPLE SAY. LAST TING I HEAH, HE UP CAYO WAY. BUT MIND YU DAT WAS AGES AGO. MAYBE EVEN YEAHS. I CANT MEMBER RIGHTLY. GOOD LUCK.'

7

Up Cayo Way

Next morning, after checking out of the Ocean Hotel, Kid bought a ticket for a bus heading out west, which would pass through the town of San Ignacio, otherwise known as Cayo. His fare only cost him six Belizean dollars – one pound fifty in English money. He marvelled that a journey right across Belize almost to the Guatemalan border could be so cheap.

A battered, yellow bus turned up and Kid found a seat next to an open window. Women selling food carried baskets up and down the aisle and, guessing that the journey might take all day, Kid bought a pie for now and another one for later.

The bus edged through the narrow streets and headed out of town. Kid dug out the note and read it again. This man whose ventures always turned to sand – was he really his father? And was he still 'up

Cayo way'? How did the writer of this note know about Kid? And why hadn't he or she left their name?

The city fell behind in a tangle of clapboard houses, cinderblock supermarkets and endless churches with exotic names. Churches, churches, churches, Kid thought – Belize seemed full of churches. Beyond the turn-off to the airport, the highway emptied save for the occasional truck roaring past, throwing up clouds of dust. Finally Kid felt that he could relax. He put away the note. There were no hostile stares to worry about any more, no hustlers wanting dollars, nobody even curious. On this bus, he was just another traveller rocking back and forth, lulled by the rhythm of the road and whatever music the driver decided to put on.

The bus passed through a flat land dotted with vegetation and occasional pools, shacks and cattle, pine ridges and little farmsteads. Mangroves sweltered in the hot sun, growing out of sandy soil. At every village, the bus turned off the highway and made a detour of pale, sandy-coloured tracks around which clustered tumble-down houses, lines of washing, broken-down old cars and banners calling on the nation to either *Believe in Belize* or *Wish for Change,* depending on the party they supported. Kid dozed until Belmopan, which he later learned was the capital of Belize, though it certainly didn't look like any capital to him. Then he slept again, only awakening when the coastal flatlands had completely gone. The bus was driving through a hilly landscape now, which was lusher and greener. The air blowing in through the windows smelt of trees, which was hardly surprising because citrus farms lined the road, their groves hanging with ripening oranges.

The people on the bus were different too, not Caribbean-looking like the ones in Belize City, but more Indian-looking and some of them speaking to each other in Spanish. One of them saw Kid staring at the oranges on the trees, and said, in slow and careful English, 'You get a chance, you pick one. Belizean oranges are as good as they look.'

Kid felt as if the journey would never end. Finally, however, the bus turned off the highway and plunged down a straight, wide road which led to a river where children were bathing. It bumped over a single-track bridge and pulled up the hill on the other side, halting beside an open market full of stalls.

'San Ignacio,' called the driver.

Kid had arrived. Getting off the bus he walked down to the back doors where people were pulling out luggage to sort out whose was whose. By the time he'd identified his rucksack, everybody else had gone. The bus pulled away and he was left alone.

Kid looked around. San Ignacio, he realised straight away, was completely different from Belize City. It wasn't just that the people here were a mix of Mestizos, speaking mostly Spanish and a form of English that he understood more easily than Kriol. It was the pace of life. No one came up to Kid or wanted anything off him, including dollars, or even bothered to look his way.

Kid started walking through the market, taking in everything from shirts to skirts, furniture to car parts, eggs and butter to vegetables and exotic fruit. No one tried to force their wares on him, and they didn't speak unless he spoke first.

Kid reached the far side of the market, crossed the road and entered a square full of shady almond trees, dotted with concrete benches painted pink and blue. Here he sat down and took stock. On one side of him was a fountain as ornamental as a wedding cake, which looked as if it had long-since been switched off. On the other side was a row of battered old taxis parked in front of a parade of shops.

One of the shops was an internet café, and Kid gave a passing moment's thought to emailing Nadine to say that he was safe and well. But beyond it was a shady bar called Mrs Edie's Place, and it looked far more inviting. Old men wandered in and seemed unwilling to come out. Dogs panted in the doorway. Women on the veranda sipped ice-cold drinks in little glasses. There were even a couple of tourists who looked as welcome as everybody else.

Kid forgot about the internet café and headed for Mrs Edie's shade instead. 'What can I get you?' called out the woman behind the bar as he picked his way between the tables.

Back at home, Kid would never have got away with it, but he tried his luck and asked for a beer. By the time he reached the bar, a chilled bottle had been opened for him and slammed on to it, wrapped in a napkin. He drank it straight down, then before the bar attendant saw how young he was and changed her mind, paid for a second one and took it to a table.

Kid drank this beer more slowly, then ordered a bottle of water and a plate of scrambled eggs. Now that he wasn't quite so thirsty, he realised how hungry he was. The eggs came with fry-jacks, which were triangles of fluffy dough deep-fried in oil. The woman brought them over. She was Mrs Edie, she said, and who was he?

Kid told her his name in full, Marcus Aurelius Cato. He hoped it would ring a bell but, if it did, she gave nothing away. She didn't even react when Kid dug out his father's photograph. Not a flicker of recognition showed in her face.

'But this man was definitely last seen up Cayo way,' Kid said, thinking that Mrs Edie looked like the sort of person who knew everybody.

'Up Cayo way doesn't just mean San Ignacio,' Mrs Edie replied. 'It's an entire district, stretching from the Guatemalan border up past Mountain Pine Ridge.'

Kid's heart sank. He showed the photo round the bar, but no one else recognised his father either. There were some comments about his mother, and some about the hat, but that was all. Had he come here on a false trail? Mrs Edie took pity on him and took a second look. The only men who ever came to town dressed as flashily as that, she said, were the ones who stayed at Night Falls Lodge.

'They might help you up there,' she said. 'They've always got strangers passing through. It's meant to be a tourist lodge but its so-called guests aren't the usual tourists, if you get my drift.'

Kid didn't get her drift, but his curiosity was aroused. What did Mrs Edie mean, he wanted to know. She muttered about night visitors and planes and something called 'Belizean breeze'. But if Kid's father was in that business, she said, he was best left well alone. In fact, she wished she hadn't mentioned Night Falls Lodge. Kid should forget she'd even spoken.

Kid tried to find out more, but Mrs Edie had already said more than enough, she reckoned, and turned her attention to her other customers. He couldn't get another word out of her. In the end, he settled up and went outside. The market was empty by now, the sun lowering and the only car on the street a taxi, its driver sitting on a low wall looking out across the square.

Kid crossed the street. A whiff of danger blew his way, but it didn't frighten him. He was up for it. 'I need a ride,' he said, his voice shaking with something that could have been fear, but he told himself it was excitement.

The driver stood up. She was a Mestizo woman with enormous hips, high, flat cheekbones and a big nose. 'I was just thinking of heading home,' she said. 'But where you wanna go?'

Kid braced himself. He knew that this was madness. He'd no real lead. No reason to hope. Only Mrs Edie's words and some crazy hunch half-forming in his brain. But he'd come to find his father, and what else had he got?

'Night Falls Lodge,' he said.

8

TAXI-MAY

The taxi driver didn't want to go that far. It was getting late, she said, and the road to Night Falls Lodge was pretty rough. It was a long way too, and she had a family wedding in the morning. Her daughter Carmelita's wedding – which meant she only had tonight to talk the stupid girl out of it, or else she'd make the biggest mistake of her life.

'Everybody knows she's making a mistake,' the driver said, 'except for her. They come to me and say Taxi-May – that's my name, Taxi-May – why's that beautiful daughter of yours marrying a man like that? She could have anyone, so why's she chosen that crook?'

She spat out the word crook. Kid said that he was sorry, but he needed to get out to Night Falls Lodge as a matter of urgency.

Taxi-May looked at him searchingly. 'You're not

in trouble, are you?' she said.

'Nothing like that,' said Kid. 'I'm just looking for someone.'

'And they can't wait till the morning?'

Kid said they couldn't. Taxi-May shook her head. 'You kids, you're all the same,' she said. 'As impatient as each other. You're like my Carmelita. If you're not in trouble yet, you will be soon, you mark my words.'

Even so, she agreed to drive Kid up as far as the Night Falls turn on the Cristo del Rey road, which was on her way home.

'But you're on your own after that,' she said. 'It'll be dark by the time we reach the turn, but you'll have to walk the rest.'

Kid didn't argue. Anything, he reckoned, beat hanging around San Ignacio knowing that he'd ignored his only lead. Taxi-May drove at breakneck speed, talking all the way, bemoaning the tragedy awaiting her daughter. She was only sixteen, apparently, and as beautiful as the sunrise. Taxi-May wanted her to get an education and make something of herself. But she'd happily see her married to anybody else, just so long as it wasn't this low-life scum.

By the time they reached the Night Falls Lodge turn, Kid knew all about it, including the fact that

Taxi-May had made the same mistake herself, apparently. She'd been sixteen too, when she'd married, and where was Carmelita's father now? Having a child had meant nothing to him, and neither had having a wife. And now here was history repeating itself.

The taxi pulled up next to a broken-down old sign announcing NIGHT FALLS LODGE. 10KM. GUESTS WELCOME. Kid opened the car door. The din of cicadas rose to greet him, and so did the same smell of trees that he'd first noticed at the airport. He started getting out, but Taxi-May dragged him back in as if she'd had second thoughts, and slammed the door.

'Talking to that daughter of mine's going to be a waste of time,' she said. 'I know that before I even start. And if you go walking off into the night, I'll end up worrying about whether you survived. It's not a park out there, in case you hadn't noticed. It's the jungle. You could get yourself eaten alive.'

She turned the taxi up the track. Kid said he didn't want to put her out and she told him to shut up. The road wound up through open farmland into rolling hills. To begin with, they drove through orange groves, with cattle grazing between the trees, white birds standing on their backs picking at them with thin, sharp beaks. But then the orange groves fell behind and Kid realised what Taxi-May had meant about jungle.

This was the landscape he'd seen from the plane, only then he'd been flying over it and now he was in the thick of it. Not only that, but night was falling fast, and there was nothing to pierce the darkness but a couple of distinctly wonky headlights.

Kid shivered and thought about Night Falls Lodge and wondered what lay ahead. Would the people up there help him? Would they recognise his father? Would they even offer him a bed for the night? Kid was a long way from town now. Taxi-May had already put herself out enough, and he didn't want to have to ask her to take him back to San Ignacio.

The road began to climb up into the hills. Taxi-May said that they were entering a dangerous region whose gorges, plunging drops and dense jungle were the perfect hideaway for smugglers and poachers.

'Are you sure you want to carry on?' she said, offering Kid a chance to turn back.

Kid shook his head. He couldn't, he said. The man he was looking for was his father, and he'd come a long way to find him – all the way from England.

Taxi-May said she hoped he knew what he was

doing. She started on about her own father and what a useless waste of space he'd been. All the while, the road was getting steeper and the car becoming slower. A cliff rose on one side of them and, in the darkness beneath them, Kid could hear the sound of a river.

Suddenly a sign loomed out of the darkness, announcing Night Falls Lodge up ahead. Beyond it, Kid caught sight of a stretch of concrete road, lit up by the taxi's headlights. They started up it, Taxi-May swearing that the damn engine would never make it to the top.

Finally, however, the car reached level ground and drew to a halt, steam seeping from its bonnet. Taxi-May switched off the engine and they sat in darkness staring at a row of thatched cabanas lit by the moon. Beyond them, Kid could make out a lawn surrounded by palms, and a cinderblock building with a tin roof, in front of which hung an illuminated sign which said RECEPTION.

He climbed out of the car. 'I'll be back in a minute to pick up my rucksack.'

'No worries. This car's not going anywhere till it's cooled down, and neither am I.'

Kid headed across the lawn. The reception door was ajar, so he pushed it open. Inside he found an office full of filing cabinets and computers, its only decoration being a jar of dead snakes pickled in gloopy liquid. The place appeared empty, but it did at least have a bell. Kid rang it and waited to see what would happen. When nothing did, he rang again. Someone had to be here, he reckoned, otherwise the lights and computers wouldn't all be on.

Finally a skinny Mestizo boy appeared, looking as surprised to see Kid as Kid was to see him.

'What you want?' he said, his voice thick with suspicion.

'This is a tourist lodge, isn't it?' Kid replied, suddenly shy about his purpose for being here. 'I'm looking for a bed for the night.'

The boy said he'd go and find somebody called Marky. It took a while for him to arrive but, when he did, he turned out to be a big, jowly bull-frog of a man with rings of armpit-sweat and a mop of bright brown hair whose colour looked highly unnatural.

'I'm pleased to see the sign down on the road is still doing its job,' he said in an accent that could have been American, but could equally have been German or Scandinavian.

Kid booked himself into a cabana. Much to his surprise, he didn't have to show his passport, and there wasn't even any register to sign, just a piece of paper.

'Here, write your name on this,' said Marky,

pushing it at him.

Kid wrote *Marcus Aurelius Cato*, then pushed the paper back, wondering if the name would mean anything. But Marky didn't even look at it. Instead he sent Kid off to Cabana No. 6 without even giving him a key, saying he wouldn't need one because, in a place like this, there were never any thefts.

'It's as safe as houses up here at Night Falls Lodge,' he said. 'We don't need keys. Everybody here's friends.'

PART THREE

BAK-A-BUSH

9

NIGHT FALLS LODGE

Taxi-May had gone when Kid finally made it back outside, leaving his rucksack on the grass. He didn't blame her, not given what she faced at home, but he missed her all the same. Standing in the dark without her, he felt as if he might just have made a terrible mistake.

Kid found Cabana No. 6, let himself in and switched on the light. It had a cool tiled floor, a high cone of thatch, shuttered windows with mosquito netting and a double bed. It was airier than the room Kid had stayed in at the Ocean Hotel, and its shower worked, as Kid quickly found out. But it smelt of mothballs, and there was dust over everything and dead flowers in a vase. Then, of course, there was the little matter of no key in the door, which mightn't matter to Marky but did to Kid.

Remembering what Taxi-May had said on the

subject of smugglers, Kid pushed a chest of drawers in front of the door and checked the fastenings on the windows. Then he lay on the bed, listening to the whirring of the electric fan and the whistling of the jungle outside, wondering whatever had possessed him to come out here. Where was his hunch now? This was crazy. Yet again he'd done what he always did. He'd done what had brought him out here to Belize. He'd acted without thinking. Acted on a whim. And look where it had got him.

The night turned cold, much to Kid's surprise. He switched off the fan, slid under the bedcovers and was just falling off to sleep when cars came labouring up the road beneath the cliff. He heard car doors banging, snatches of voices and laughter. Then, later on, he heard the pounding drums of punta rock, Belize's favourite music, which carried on for most of the night.

Night Falls Lodge mightn't be the obvious place to a hold a party, but one was definitely being held. Every time Kid awoke, it was still on the go. Only in the morning did silence fall. Kid opened the wooden shutters and looked out. All the cars had gone, leaving behind a grey, empty lawn surrounded by trees shrouded in mist. It was as if the party had never taken place.

Kid pulled on some clothes and went outside,

shocked to find out how warm it was so early in the day. What he hoped he'd find he'd no idea, but someone to talk to wouldn't have gone amiss. He sauntered across the lawn, heading for an open-sided structure with a thatched roof, which looked as if it had once been a restaurant, but not any more. A bright green parrot swooped into it from one side and went out the other. Kid walked between tables piled with chairs. Another smaller bird hovered over a blossom growing up in the thatch, and Kid realised it was a humming-bird.

Suddenly a boy appeared, the same sort of age as the one Kid had met last night. He pulled the chairs off a table and started laying it. Breakfast was on the way, he said.

No sooner had he finished than a sun-leathered man appeared as well, as thin as a rake and smelling like the inside of a tobacco tin. Saying 'Hi' in an accent straight off the cowboy movies, he sat down opposite Kid and poured them both a coffee out of little tin jug.

Instinctively Kid didn't like this man. He shivered. The man's mouth was smiling but his eyes were cold. When another boy brought out two plates of scrambled eggs, he snapped at him for being so slow. And when he started eating, he cursed the boy because the eggs weren't cooked to his liking.

The boy had to bring out fresh eggs while the man sat back and sipped his coffee, which was black and bitter, Kid discovered, when he tried his own. Then, after the eggs, the boy brought out plates of sliced fruit, including pineapples, bananas, guavas and papaya – all grown here on what he called 'Mistah Marky's farm'. The American gave him a look as if he was talking too much, and the boy's smile dried up.

He slunk away. As soon as he'd gone, the American said, 'You sleep okay, did you? You weren't disturbed by the noise? These are historic times, y'know. It was election day yesterday. The boys were up celebrating their new government. They been waiting years for it and now they're hoping everything's gonna change.'

He chuckled as if he personally new better. His name was Dave, he said, and he'd been living out here – bak-a-bush, as he called it – for years. Anything Kid wanted to know about the jungle, Dave was his man. In fact, anything Kid wanted to know about Belize in general, Dave was his man.

'What you doin' round these parts?' he asked. 'You're not Belizean, are you? What's brought you here?'

Here was Kid's chance to talk about his father. But something about Dave made him hold back.

'I'm on holiday,' he said. 'I come from England. I'm a tourist.'

It didn't sound true somehow and Kid guessed from Dave's expression that he didn't quite believe it. He started pressing him about what sort of tourist and from where, but a voice called him away. Kid watched him ambling off, and felt relieved. He finished his breakfast and went looking for Marky. He was the man in charge. If anyone had any knowledge about Kid's father it was most likely to be him.

Kid crossed the lawn to reception, but Marky was nowhere to be seen. In fact, the whole place seemed deserted. Even the boys had disappeared. Kid looked in the kitchen, which lay behind reception, but no one was there so he headed off round the garden.

Kid explored the entire grounds, but didn't see a soul, not even another guest. At one point, he ended up by the river. Another time he found himself on the edge of the jungle, with trees closing in around him. Finally, way beyond the far side of the lawn, he came across a swimming pool, deserted like everywhere else but at least full of water.

The day was heating up by now, so Kid decided to take a dip. There were leaves on the surface of the water, but that didn't bother him. He dived in, to find the water cool and wonderful. After swimming a couple of lengths, he flipped over and floated on his back. Maybe he hadn't found Marky, but this went some way to making up for it.

Only when Dave appeared did Kid think about getting out. Another man accompanied him, who looked nothing like a tourist. The two of them headed for an open-air bar situated on the far side of the pool and Kid wondered if the man was one of last night's partygoers.

He swam on, trying to ignore them both. But it was difficult. Voices drifted his way, going on about the sorts of opportunities the new government would bring, and the money that could be made. Then Marky appeared out of nowhere and joined in. The stranger was going on about a patch of land he was thinking of buying down Placencia way, where the tourist boom was really taking off. But Marky said he had land round here to sell, and Dave the American said he did as well.

'There's oil here in this ground,' he said, 'waiting to be found. It doesn't take a Texan to smell *that* one out.'

Marky and Dave the American glanced at each other. It was obvious to Kid that they had plans of their own, regardless of what they might be saying. He shivered, imagining his father being in this stranger's shoes, a businessman maybe, but no match for a pair like Marky and Dave.

By now Kid had stopped swimming and it was hard to hide the fact that he was listening in. Dave came sauntering over with an opened Belikin beer, which he handed to Kid, saying it was free on the house.

'How long did you say you were staying?' he asked.

Kid flushed as if caught out and said he didn't know. Dave looked at him with cold eyes.

'If you're feeling at a loose end,' he said, 'we could always fix up a tourist trip. There are deep dark caves nearby, which we could lose you in, or rapids in the river where you could risk life and limb. Hang around long enough and *we'll fix something up.*'

It sounded more like a threat than a tourist opportunity. Kid felt himself turn cold all over. The American walked away, as thin and mean as an alley-cat, and Kid asked himself what he was doing here, irritating these people by getting under their feet. He swam a couple more lengths to prove – to himself as much as anyone – that he wasn't scared. Then he went back to his cabana where he pushed the chest of drawers in front of the door and started packing. Something definitely was wrong about this place. Mrs Edie had been right when she'd called its so-called guests unlikely tourists, and Taxi-May had been right when she'd said that his impatience would get him into trouble.

Kid went looking for Marky to settle up. He returned to the pool, but Marky had gone. Went back to reception, but he wasn't there. Tried the kitchen again but he wasn't there, and the boys didn't know where he was, and they'd never heard of a man called Marcus Aurelius Cato.

Finally Kid ended up down by the river again, though goodness only knew why. He stopped to watch kingfishers scudding over sunlit waters and spirals of butterflies dancing round each other. It was lovely here, quiet and still. He sat on a small sandy beach wishing he didn't have to go back to the lodge. Gradually he fell asleep. His sleepless night caught up on him, and so did the heat of the day. He stayed asleep for hours too, lulled by the sound of the river flowing past.

When Kid awoke, the sun was coming down the sky and he knew that if he intended to head back to San Ignacio part of his journey would be walked in the dark. Even so, he was still determined to leave. At least he was until he bumped into Marky halfway up the steps leading back to the lodge.

'You still here?' said Marky. 'Well, supper's ready. I've cooked it myself tonight, so it's good grub.

Come and eat.'

It sounded like a command. Kid wouldn't have dared do anything other than follow Marky to the veranda at the back of his office, where a table had been laid. Some jangly pop music was playing on the radio and geckos were scuttling up and down the walls like tiny grey ghosts. A girl brought out a tray full of drinks, followed by one of the boys with plates of nameless meat served in a shiny, thick brown gravy.

Kid ate it all, but it wasn't easy, especially with a thin black snake, coiled on a beam above his head, making occasional lunges at the geckos who shrieked in anguish as they tried to get away. Kid's father's photograph sat in his back pocket, but he never got round to showing it because Dave turned up with two new guests, pretending they were tourists, though Kid didn't believe a word of it.

After supper, the night warmed up. One of the guests produced a bottle of tequila to drink the health of the new government, and the girl who'd brought out the drinks came and danced for them, shaking her body to a punta rock drumbeat, and driving her hips in a way that had even Kid blushing, who'd witnessed Nadine in action. She wore a peppermint-green skirt that hugged her hips and flew out around her as she danced. Seeing Kid watching her, she called for him to come and join her. But he shook his head, and everybody laughed.

One of the guests started to his feet instead. But before he could get anywhere near the girl, a great brown bullfrog – which looked just like Marky, Kid thought – hopped on to the veranda and drove the girl away. Everybody laughed as she ran shrieking into the kitchen, slamming the door behind her. The guest looked disappointed, but Marky said he was wasting his time anyway.

'Belizean women are pretty enough when they're young,' he said. 'But as they start getting older, they get bellies on them.'

He was one to talk, Kid thought. He glanced around the table, where everyone was smirking as if thinking the same thing. Then Dave broke the silence, asking Kid about his plans tomorrow and how long he intended to stay around.

Everybody leant forward, as if they all wanted to know. Kid knew he should tell them what they obviously wanted to hear – that he'd be out first thing and wouldn't ever be back. But something got hold of him – madness, foolhardiness, maybe even cussedness. Or maybe it was just plain curiosity to see what would happen next.

'I've got no plans,' Kid said – and never had a truer word been uttered. 'I thought tomorrow I'd just chill out.'

Silence greeted this. Then Dave and his guests rose to their feet, saying they thought they'd turn in early, and Marky said he had things to attend to in the office and suddenly the party was over.

Kid returned to his cabana, fully understanding how much trouble he'd landed himself in. He pushed the chest back in front of his door, then every other piece of furniture as well, including the bed. What had got into him? These people were desperate to get rid of him. They were up to something, plainly enough, and his being around was interfering with their plans. Belizean breeze, Mrs Edie had said – well, it didn't take much imagination to guess what *that* might be.

'Why didn't I just give them what they wanted? After all, it's what I want as well. No way do I want to chill out here. Why've I got to be so hard on myself?'

Kid was still trying to work it all out when someone knocked on the door.

'Mistah Cato,' a voice whispered, 'Mistah Marcus Cato, are you there? I want to talk to you . . .'

It was the girl. The one with the peppermint-green skirt. Kid was so shocked to hear her call him by his father's name that he pulled back the furniture and let her in. She sat on the bed with her back against his rucksack. She was his friend, she said. He could tell her anything. She wasn't like them, not like Marky or Dave.

'What are you *really* doing here?' she asked. 'Everybody wants to know, but I won't let on. I hate them all. I never tell them anything. I'm good at secrets. *You can tell me anything.*'

This last was almost whispered. The girl leant forward. She smelt of flowers. Kid leant forward too. Maybe it was her closeness, or his own sense of relief to have a friend in this place, but he suddenly felt the longing to talk. He was looking for his father, he said and the whole story came out, starting with one Marcus Aurelius Cato and ending with the other. Had the girl ever heard of him? Kid wanted to know. The word in San Ignacio was that he might have been up here. Had the girl seen him? Did she know him? Could she remember anybody like this man ever passing through?

Kid showed her the photograph. The girl looked at it, but said nothing. Kid could see her thinking hard. She was hiding something. He was sure of it.

'If I told you that this man came through here once, ages ago, but I don't know who he is and he never came back, would that do?' she said at last.

Kid felt a chill run up his spine. The girl *was* hiding something. He knew she was. But then that's what everybody had been doing – not just her or Marky or Mistah Dave, but the person who'd written that note back in Belize City, and even his mother, who had hidden his father from him for years.

'The only way I'm leaving,' he said, 'is if you tell me where he went. And, if you won't, I'll call in the police.'

The girl shivered. Kid feared that his words had been a big mistake but, much to his surprise, they seemed to do the trick. 'Well, in that case,' she said with a sigh, 'I've got no choice, have I? Seeing as you're determined to know, your father's alive and well, at least he was last time I saw him. He lives on a piece of land up-river, which he bought off Marky because it's full of gold. He and Marky fell out over it. Marky said your father cheated him, and he's so angry about it that he won't allow his name to be mentioned, which means I'd be in big trouble if he could hear me now.'

All of this was delivered in one single breath. The girl looked at Kid with huge, worried eyes.

'Gold,' Kid said.

'Gold,' she replied. 'Belize is full of it. The Macal River in particular. You only have to scoop up the riverbed and you've got handfuls of the stuff.'

The two of them sat in the darkness, their faces

almost touching. Kid tried to imagine not only finding his father, but finding him *rich*. A picture came into his head of the big white house he'd imagined back in England, with servants, lawns and a pool. Where exactly was this place? he demanded to know.

The girl said it could be found out on the Cristo del Rey road, but the easiest way to get to it from Night Falls Lodge was straight up-river. It would only take an hour or so, a couple at the most.

'What, through the jungle?' Kid said.

'If you're man enough,' the girl said, 'there's nothing to it. All you have to do is stick to the river-bank. Anyone with half a sense could do that.'

Kid felt himself flush at this insult to his pride. What was his father like? he wanted to know. His heart pounded at the thought of meeting him. Until this moment, he realised he'd never really believed that this would happen.

The girl looked completely at a loss for words. 'He's just a man,' she said. 'I don't know.'

But Kid persisted. What *sort* of man, he insisted.

The girl shrugged. 'People come and go at Night Falls Lodge,' she said. 'Sometimes you learn their names, sometimes you don't. Sometimes you get to know them but, even though your father wasn't one of those, I saw enough to know that, if he was my father, I'd be up that river after him before Marky could stop me. Because he will, you know. *So I'd get out of here while you still can.*

10

A WHOLE WORLD OF DIFFERENCE

Kid did just that. He slipped away first thing, before Marky was about, leaving his rucksack behind in the interests of travelling light. He also left a note saying he'd be back for it, then packed his valuables, including his passport, parents' photograph and mother's hat, into his day-bag, along with a bottle of water and some fruit sneaked from the kitchen.

Then Kid set off, feeling like a proper explorer. Nadine should see me now, he thought, as he headed down to the Macal River. Jet should see his burger-boy. Kyle should see his boots in action. The day was fresh and the air still, not a hint of a movement except for the occasional bird startled out of the trees as Kid walked past. A short way up-river, he came to a series of falls which he guessed gave the lodge its name. Here he came across a little man standing on a stony beach watering his horse. He was the smallest man Kid had ever seen and his presence, at such an early hour, was totally unexpected.

The man watched Kid approach. Where was he going, he wanted to know. Up-river? Then where was his guide? Where was his equipment and where his map? Had he brought a compass? And what about provisions? A bottle of water and a bit of fruit? Did he really think that was good enough? Didn't Kid know that there were untold dangers out here bak-a-bush? Running out of food and water would be the least of his problems if he carried on as he was. There were wild peccary out here, who'd charge as soon as look at you, and jaguars who'd tear you limb from limb. There were snakes too – including deadly coral snakes and fer-de-lances that you wouldn't see until they leapt – and poisonous trees that could kill you at a single scratch.

Not only that, but there were *brujos* in the forest, the old man said – the spirits of evil people who took on the form of wild beasts and haunted the jungle looking for prey.

'If you show them that you're scared, you'll end up dead,' the old man said. 'And you will be scared, believe me.'

Kid thanked the man for his advice, but explained that he wasn't mounting a major expedition, just taking a short walk up-river to his father's place. His father, the gold miner Marcus Aurelius Cato. Had the man heard of him?

The man said he hadn't, but that that meant nothing because he'd never been any good at names. It was what people did that counted, he said, not what they called themselves. He mounted his horse and turned to set off. By the way, this wasn't a jungle, he said. It was a forest. There was a whole world of difference. Most people didn't seem to realise that.

The man rode away, pulling a hat down over his head and whistling a song to himself, which quickly faded amid the other whirrs and whistles of the forest. Kid resumed his journey too. The way seemed harder after that. In order to remain close to the river, he had to dodge vines, step over fallen logs and push his way between branches. This was no nature trail with well-cut paths and way marks. Jungle, forest or simply bak-a-bush, this was a place where nature ran wild.

It was also a place where silence reigned, for all the forest's surface chatter. Strange-sounding birds called to each other from tree to tree, but they never disturbed that silence; it was always there. Branches hung over the river, creating pools of shadow amid the growing brightness of the day. Kid saw clouds of brightly coloured butterflies and bright green parrots. Exquisite perfume wafted his way and he looked up to see exotic blossoms growing overhead.

Slowly Kid began to see why the little man had called this place a forest, not a jungle. This wasn't just a wild, dense scrub. It was a place of sunlight, shade and incredible trees. A patchwork of light and darkness. A place of growth and extraordinary life.

Every time Kid found a stretch of river with a beach, he plunged in to cool off. The water was crystal-clear and shone like gold. Kid wished that he could bottle it and take it away. He wished that he could bottle the whole forest, every last tree.

The sun rose higher all the time and the day grew hotter. Kid's pace began to drag. His day-bag started digging into his shoulders. It mightn't have much in it, but it began to feel as if it weighed a tonne. Round every bend in the river, Kid looked with anticipation as if he expected to find his father in the river panning for gold. An hour went by, then a second one and then a third. But there was never any sign of him, or of his house.

There were plenty of other signs of life, though. Signs of ant life, termite life, bird life, bee life, spider life, frog life, even great spiky iguana life. Once Kid almost fell into a termites' nest. Another time he stopped to rest right in the middle of a column of tree-cutter ants. Then he disturbed some bees and had to shelter in the river.

But even so, Kid was full of hope, and he remained that way all morning. It was only after lunch, when his water bottle had emptied and he'd eaten all his fruit, that his hopes began to fade. The girl had said two hours, but he'd been on his feet all day. Not only that but, if he didn't turn about soon, he wouldn't get back before darkness fell.

'Another hour,' Kid told himself. 'I've come too far to turn back yet. I'll press on a bit longer.'

In an hour's time, however, Kid had still not found his father's place. He'd somehow managed to lose the river, however, and the forest had become so dark and overgrown that he could scarcely see where he was going. Plainly no one but him had been here for years, not even to indulge in a little light gold-mining.

Kid finally gave in and started picking his way back. He didn't want to, but the day was drawing to a close and he knew he had no choice. By now the forest floor was so overgrown that Kid couldn't even see where he was putting his feet. In the trees somewhere a noise started up which he'd heard last night in his cabana, and the girl had said was made by howler monkeys.

It sounded more like roaring jaguars to Kid. Hungry jaguars on the prowl. He turned away in a panic, forcing a path between the trees, certain that the sound was coming after him. And suddenly, right in front of him, he found a house.

Kid stood and gawped. The house was covered with vines and creepers, and it was plainly in ruins. Its roof had half fallen in, its stairs were broken and its balcony in tatters. Was it his father's house – the one that he'd been looking for? If not, whose was it? And why was it in ruins? What had happened here? And, if it was his father's house, then where was he? What had happened to him?

For a moment Kid couldn't bring himself to move, then cautiously he started picking his way up the broken stairs and across the balcony. Common sense said that the owner of this property, whoever he might be, couldn't possibly be inside. But a crazy hope rose inside of Kid.

'Hello,' he called. 'Is anybody there? Marcus Aurelius Cato . . . Father . . . Dad . . .?'

There was no reply. Scorpions scuttled across the balcony and bees hummed in the remains of the thatch. Kid stooped beneath a broken door-frame and entered a single room with bare boards, a table and the remains of an old stove, including a broken chimney pipe. Saplings grew up through the floor-boards. The room had plainly been uninhabited for a long time, except for the scuttling presence of the biggest beetles Kid had ever seen.

He picked his way across the floor, hoping that he wouldn't fall through. On the beam above the table, he found a jar of salt, a couple of dust-encrusted spoons and a stack of plastic plates. On the table he found the remains of what he guessed were rotted teabags in a jar, and a stack of rusted tins of food. On the stove he found the clean white remains of what appeared to be animal bones.

But Kid found nothing personal in that room. Whoever had once lived here had left behind nothing of themselves. There were no pictures. No personal belongings. And, most definitely, there was no father.

Kid stood in the middle of the floor, surrounded by life that had no regard for whoever had lived here, but carried on its own sweet way. Never had he felt so small and insignificant. Here the forest had taken over and the minor human drama of himself and his father simply didn't count.

Kid scouted round one last time, but all he found was the remains of heavy drinking. Out on the balcony, he walked across a carpet of broken bottles, and back inside again, dust-laden on a beam, he discovered a half-drunk bottle of whisky. Not rum. Not Belikin beer. But Scotch whisky.

Kid had never liked Scotch. It had been his mother's favourite drink. But now he unscrewed the bottle and downed the lot, not caring what it did to him.

After that, a wild, crazy rage got hold of him. That girl at Night Falls Lodge had known what she was doing, hadn't she? His coming to this place had been no mistake. She'd tempted him, goaded him, pricked at his pride and done everything she could to get him out of Night Falls Lodge. That was why she'd turned up, knocking on his door. She'd been sent by Dave and Marky to sit on his bed, smelling of flowers, calling herself his friend, wheedling secrets out of him and getting rid of him by telling lies about a man she'd no doubt never met.

Well, if she wanted to get rid of me, she certainly succeeded, Kid thought. They all have. *Look how well they've done!*

Kid wept at what he'd come so close to finding, only to fail. He wept for whoever's place this was, his father's or some stranger's – it made no difference, because what a way to end up. And, after that, there was no hope for him. He found a stash of rum and drank that too – or at least as much as he could before it knocked him out. Later he awoke to find himself in pitch darkness, something crawling over him. He lay and let it happen, not caring what it was. Jaguar, fer-de-lance, even those *brujos* the little old man had told him about – he didn't care.

Kid closed his eyes. He didn't feel cold. Didn't feel hungry or thirsty. Most of all, he didn't feel afraid.

'I'm not scared, so don't you think I am,' he whispered – though he didn't know who to. 'Whatever happens next is fine. It's all fine. Everything. See if I care.'

11

AT THE BRIDGE

Kid slept deeply after that. The alcohol did that for him at least. He awoke next morning, still alive though feeling like death. Somehow, he knew, he had to find his way back to Night Falls Lodge, retrieve his rucksack and get out of there before his anger at what Marky, Dave and that wretched, lying girl had done to him finally spilled over and he did something he'd regret.

It took a while before Kid could move but finally, day-bag over his shoulders, he stumbled out of the house and down to the river. It was absurdly easy to find. How he'd lost it yesterday he didn't know. He set off along it and walked until time meant nothing any more, and all that mattered was the next step. His head throbbed, his stomach gnawed with hunger and his body ran with sweat. Occasionally the way was shady but increasingly the forest opened out, exposing the river to the sun.

By now, Kid's feet had formed blisters thanks to Kyle's new boots, and his legs were aching so much that even standing still was painful. He tried to create a pattern to his walking – to build a sense of rhythm. But the heat was getting to him and he simply couldn't think. He should have stopped to drink, filling his empty water bottle from the river, but he couldn't even organise himself to do that.

Things weren't making sense any more, not like yesterday when, however tired he'd been, Kid had managed to think straight. Sometimes his brain was so fuddled that it seemed to him that he was walking backwards. Once he swore that he could see himself ahead on the track. Another time he imagined that he could see Kyle on the track.

Something really weird was happening inside Kid's head. Another time he saw his mother looking hot and weary. She wiped the hair out of her eyes and whispered that she was looking for his father too. Kid whispered back, asking her how she'd managed to return to life. But, before she could answer, a crowd of people suddenly appeared.

Something was definitely wrong here. Kid's mother disappeared, like Kyle had done before her, and Kid was left with the people, who were walking up and down a low stone bridge with the river running beneath it. All of them were white-skinned, older than him by a couple of years, he guessed, and calling out to each other in unmistakably English accents. Some were wearing nothing but underwear. Others were jumping off the bridge into the river, where they splashed and swam about. The bridge and river were swarming with them. Some even sunbathed right there in the middle of the bridge, oiling their bodies, and the girls shaving their legs.

Kid felt as if he'd walked straight out of the jungle into the Costa del Sol. If he'd ever doubted that he was losing his mind, he now knew it for sure. Nervously he moved towards the bridge, terrified of what these weird, unreal people might do to him, but unable to stop. Things started swaying. All around him, the sun was bleaching everything white.

Kid reached the bridge, hauled himself up on to it and stood waiting to see what would happen next. Nobody took much notice of him. It was as if he was the person who wasn't real, not everybody else. A blonde-haired girl called for him to hand over her towel, and he was relieved that at least somebody could see him. At least he hadn't imagined himself.

'Are you all right there?' the girl said. 'You look really hot. You should take a dip as well. And you could do with a drink, by the looks of things.

Though I'd hurry up if I was you. We haven't got much longer. Looks like Jez is waiting.'

She nodded down the bridge. Kid followed her glance. To add to everything else that couldn't possibly be real, he saw a convoy of Land Rovers stretching off into the jungle, their roof racks piled with equipment. Having dried her hair, the girl started heading towards them. Kid staggered after her, shaking his head in disbelief. She didn't question his presence, which was really weird, but then neither did anybody else. Even when Kid followed the girl into the back of the nearest Land Rover, she didn't question him. Other people piled in too and he waited to be thrown out. But, apart from complaining about how crushed they were, nobody said a thing.

The Land Rovers set off, everybody cheering to be on their way. Kid sat rigid with fear, reckoning that the jungle had finally done for him and he'd gone mad. On one side of him sat a thin, pale-skinned Goth with two straight sheets of dyed black hair. On the other sat the blonde girl, who answered to the name Snow. Snow in Belize! It was just about as crazy as everything else.

Kid closed his eyes, expecting everyone to be gone when he opened them again. A conversation started up. The Goth boy was called Jack. A curly-haired joker next to him answered to the name of Fritz. A voice on the other side of Kid came from someone called Hal. But even if they had names, these people couldn't be real, Kid told himself. This simply wasn't happening. They were going on now about some jungle training they'd been doing at a place called Gallon Jug, which was where they'd all first met. Whoever heard of a place named that?

Kid fell asleep, weary, hot and confused. When he awoke again, the convoy was pulling into a forest clearing. Land Rover doors banged open and people piled out. Kid followed them. The first thing he noticed was that the trees pressing in around the clearing were completely different from those around Night Falls Lodge – taller and somehow more majestic. But there was nothing majestic about the clearing itself. It was littered with great hulking pieces of what looked like earth-moving machinery, and the ground was bare and muddy where vehicles had passed through.

'Welcome to Millionaros,' said one of the group's leaders, a wiry, taut man called Jez. 'The old man says we can brew up on his fire, so who's got the tea?'

The old man in question was the owner of the only dwelling in the clearing – a corrugated-tin shack held together by sheets of tarpaulin. He lived here all alone with nothing but his fire for company. Once he'd had dogs, but the jaguars had eaten them. His job, apparently, was to guard the machinery which belonged to a mining company.

Kid's ears pricked up when he heard that. What sort of mining, he wondered, just as the other leader of the group – a tiny, plaited woman whose name was Candy – told them it was gold.

'In fact, that's where we're heading,' she said. 'Up to a place called Gold Mine. We won't get there tonight, but we should tomorrow, unless anything goes wrong. On foot, of course – by then we'll have long since left the Land Rovers behind.'

Kid didn't care about the Land Rovers. Candy was going on about the trek ahead and how hard it was going to be, but all he could think about was the gold mine. What if it was his father's one, and that girl back at Night Falls Lodge hadn't lied after all, except in minimising the distances involved? The hope that had died in Kid sprang back to life. He determined to stay with the group for as long as he could get away with it.

Kid was the first back into the Land Rover when Jez said it was time to move on. Everybody packed in behind him and still no questions were asked. By now the last semblances of a track had been left behind and the Land Rovers pitched an increasingly difficult path through one muddy bog after another. People wondered out loud about what lay ahead. The word *xateros* was mentioned, referring to armed bandits. They could be anywhere, apparently, moving through the forest like shadows, so many of them that beyond Gold Mine, deeper in the jungle, the group would have to be guarded by soldiers.

Finally the Land Rovers reached a point where they could pitch and roll no further. Everybody piled out into the mud, and all the expedition equipment had to be transferred on to their backs. Kid was given a heavy rucksack full of foodstuff, which made him stagger just standing still. He could sense how nervous people were all around him. This was it, they were thinking. This isn't jungle training – it's the real thing.

A line formed on the muddy track, and Kid positioned himself at the rear, keeping his head down. Maybe the group had made the mistake of thinking he was one of them, but the leaders wouldn't and he didn't want them noticing him. The others started off, marching along a boggy track gouged out of the forest by gold-mine machinery. Kid followed them, the sun beating down on his head. Right from the word go, he found it difficult keeping up. In the last couple of days, he'd done enough jungle trekking to last a lifetime. Even before starting to trek again, he was hot, weary, tired, and suffering from dehydration.

But every time he faltered, Kid thought about his father up ahead. His rich father with the white house and the swimming pool. His father who was waiting to welcome him with open arms. At least, he hoped he was.

'Are you all right?' asked the girl in front of Kid, a fiery-looking red-head whose name was Joanne.

Kid said that he was fine, and forced himself on. But sweat was pouring down him and he'd long-since lost all sense of time. How long had he been walking? He didn't know. How many breaks had he taken? He didn't know. How far had he come? He didn't know anything except that somewhere ahead of him, drawing closer all the time, was his father, his father, his father . . .

The track became muddier, but Kid didn't care. He was beyond all that. Sometimes it was possible to get round the mud, but sometimes he had to wade through it, sticking like glue, sucking at his boots. Increasingly he found it difficult to lift his legs. Finally, he keeled over. His whole world up-ended, he felt himself go and he didn't even care. None of this was real anyway. Only Gold Mine was real. Everything else was a pale, fading dream.

Kid came to himself face down in the mud,

unable to figure out how he'd got there or how to get up. He realised he must have blacked out, because people were around him who hadn't been there before. Arms tried lifting him, and shrill voices said things he couldn't grasp until Jez's voice cut through them all.

'These things happen. Get the lad some water. Give him space. Who is he? Whose Land Rover was he in? Candy, is he one of yours? *Can someone tell me this lad's name?*'

Silence greeted this request and, in that silence, Kid knew he'd been found out. He felt himself being lifted out of the mud and his face being swabbed with water. A bottle was pressed to his mouth. He took a couple of gulps, then a couple more, then the bottle was empty somehow and a new one was being pressed to his mouth. Then everything started going again in a tangle of faces and trees. Kid saw bright lights. Then he saw nothing.

When Kid came round again – came round properly, that is, instead of existing in some half-dreaming state where he felt himself being carried but wasn't really sure that he was there – the track had gone, and so had all the mud, and he was lying on a stony beach with a river flowing over him. Nothing in his life had ever felt so good. Slowly he lifted his head. The beach was made up of small, honey-coloured pebbles. Kid wasn't imagining it. It was completely real. Completely there in front of him, and Jez was real as well. No one else was there except for the two of them and the birds in the trees and the river flowing past.

'Better?' Jez said when Kid dragged himself up into sitting position.

'Much better,' Kid said. 'How did I get here?'

'Good question, that,' Jez said.

Kid felt himself flush. Jez looked like a man not to be messed with. He stared at Kid and Kid stared back, then Jez asked him, quietly but very firmly, how he'd managed to attach himself to the group, where he'd done it and, for God's sake, why.

Jez wanted the whole story. 'Where do you come from?' he said. 'A young kid like you, all on your own. And what are you doing here? You do know you're in the Chiquibul Forest where no one's allowed without a government pass. This isn't just any ordinary forest, you know. It's a protected forest full of jaguars and endangered trees. You may not know it, but you've walked straight into one of the last great forests of the Americas.'

Kid told him his whole story. There was something about Jez that demanded nothing less. He started with his mother's cardboard box and ended with trying to find his father up at Night Falls

Lodge. Normally Kid never gave much about himself away but, for reasons he couldn't explain, his story felt safe with Jez. Maybe it was the place that made him feel like that. The sense of absolute peace. Kid even told Jez about his mother's hat.

'You mean you came into the jungle without anything useful for your survival, but you brought *that*?' Jez said when Kid pulled it out to show him.

Kid felt a fool. 'Not only that,' Jez said, 'but you've been drinking. Don't tell me that you haven't because you've been sweating alcohol. I can smell it.'

Kid hung his head. 'I don't know what to say,' he said.

'Well, come back into camp when you're ready, and we'll decide what to do about you,' Jez said.

He left Kid on his own, watching the river flowing past. Trees tumbled down to it, its steep banks bright with exotic flowers. Upstream, an enormous arch of honey-coloured limestone hung over the water, its reflection in its glassy surface creating a perfect circle. Stalactites hung under the arch and, his curiosity aroused, Kid waded into the river to take a closer look at them.

Suddenly, however, the river-bed fell away from him and he found himself plunged into deep water and thrashing about. The water was clear and he could see fish darting about beneath the surface.

Regaining his composure, he swam under the arch, then flipped over and floated on his back staring up at the stalactites.

They hung above his head, great red-and-honey-coloured spikes. Beyond the arch, Kid could see the jungle alive with every shade of green from emerald to aquamarine. The sun was bright out there. He caught flashes of turquoise, yellow and red as birds dipped and skimmed across the surface of the water. So many colours in one place. So much to see. So much to drink in.

Finally Kid flipped over and swam back into the sunlight. Here he cut through the glassy water, taking his time for once – which had to be a first for a boy like him – not acting impulsively, but taking slow, deliberate strokes, one after another, which was the best way of doing things if you wanted to keep afloat.

12

GOLD MINE

Doc Rose appeared just as Kid was coming up from the water. She didn't look old enough to be a doctor, but she certainly knew her stuff. When she'd finished examining Kid from head to toe, she explained about the side-effects of dehydration and the dangers of mixing sun, alcohol and a chronic lack of water. Then, for good measure, she sorted out Kid's blisters, put powder between his toes and gave him a lecture on the threat of trench foot if he didn't take better care.

When she'd finished lecturing Kid, the two of them made their way up to a forest clearing where the group was camped for the night. A fire had been lit and people were either cooking supper, stringing up their hammocks, or lying in them, writing up their diaries. There was no sign of Jez or Candy, but Doc Rose said they were off somewhere, setting up their aerial to report back to Craig, the field manager of their organisation, about picking up a spare.

Kid said he'd been called a few things in his life, but never *a spare*. 'What's Jez going to do about me?' he asked.

'It depends on Craig,' Doc Rose replied. 'My guess is that he'll agree for you to stay with us until we reach our destination at Rio Blanco. After all, no one can be spared to trek you out before then. We're carrying too much vital equipment for anyone to turn back. And no way could you trek out of here on your own.'

When Jez came back, he said the same thing almost word for word. 'Which means you're stuck with us,' he said to Kid. 'At least you are for the next few days. But then we're stuck with you as well – so I suggest you give some thought to how you can make yourself useful.'

Over supper, Kid was officially introduced to the rest of the group – though Jez kept the personal details to himself, simply describing Kid as an example of what could happen if one entered the jungle unprepared. People stared at Kid as if he'd landed from another planet, and he stared back warily. These people weren't figments of his imagination, after all. They were real live Jaydene Lewis rich-kid types. Up-themselves, do-good types. Gap-year volunteers.

But, no matter what Kid thought of them, when donations were sought to provide him with a jungle kit, Kid found the group generous to a fault, handing over spare head-torches, mess tins, foot powder, iodine, penknives, Deet to keep off the mosquitoes, and a belt-kit. Someone even found a sleeping bag they didn't want, and Candy handed over the group's emergency spare hammock, complete with mosquito net and Basha sheet, and asked someone to help Kid put it up.

The boy who helped Kid was the one called Hal. When anything irritated him his face went a dull red. And Kid's inability to grasp the basics of stringing up a hammock really irritated him. 'That's not high enough,' he kept saying. 'That's not tight enough . . . Those strings will come undone . . . You haven't fixed the mosquito net right . . .'

Kid had to start again several times over, with Hal standing over him acting the jungle expert, though really he was nothing but a fresh-faced farmer's son from Shropshire, who'd only arrived in Belize a week or so ago. Even when the hammock was right, Hal insisted that its green nylon Basha 'roof' was in the wrong place, and then he complained that the mosquito net was trailing on the ground and would pick up bugs.

When Kid had finally got everything right, Hal demonstrated how to climb into a hammock without falling straight out. He made it look easy, but when Kid attempted it, he crashed straight on to the ground. It took four times to get it right, and attracted quite an audience. Finally, though, Kid got the knack of it and wriggled down his sleeping bag – though with his mosquito net tucked round him he didn't dare move.

Everybody laughed at him lying there like that, strung up between trees, unable to make himself comfortable. Even Hal couldn't help but laugh. Snow was there, and Fritz the joker of the group, who later turned Kid's efforts into a funny song. There was a boy wearing a *Star Wars* T-shirt, whose name was Al, and the black-haired boy who Kid nicknamed Jack-the-Goth.

Kid reckoned he liked Snow, but wasn't sure about the rest. She was Dutch, although her English was perfect. Joanne – the girl who'd stood behind Kid on the trek – came from Cardiff in Wales. Fritz was a boarding-school boy, who said he didn't come from anywhere, whatever *that* meant. And Hal was a country boy, as he kept telling everyone, having grown up on what he called 'God's own earth'.

Some of the group were on their gap year

between school and university. Most of them had never left home before. All of them – including Hal, in Kid's estimation – were clueless about how to look after themselves out in the real world.

That night, Kid lay awake wondering how he was going to survive these people for another day. He thought about his father up at Gold Mine, and pulled out his mystery note to read it again. He had a head-torch to read with, but he could have done it anyway because the moon was so bright, shining down upon the camp.

Kid pulled his newly acquired sleeping bag round him. He felt safe in the trees, swinging gently in his hammock, strung up between the branches where nothing could get him. Safer – if he was honest with himself – than he'd felt back in London with police sirens going off every few minutes and all Nadine's locks and chains on the front door.

Diamonds of light looked down at Kid from the trees all around the clearing as hidden creatures watched him. Did his eyes sparkle back, he wondered? And what did those creatures make of him? Distantly he heard howler monkeys roaring and remembered mistaking the sound for the roar of jaguars. So much had happened since then. After what he'd been through, Kid felt like a different person.

The roaring grew closer until it reached the

camp, its calls echoing from one side to the other, high up in the trees. Kid lay in his hammock, eyes wide open, hoping that he'd see something. For a few moments the unforgettable, full-throated roars of howler monkeys hurtled at each other from the trees on one side of the camp to the trees on the other. Then the roars started fading, and slowly the performance drew to a close. The howlers faded into the night, leaving behind not a swaying branch or a rustling leaf.

Next morning, Kid found himself on the rota to help to cook porridge for more people than he could count. Afterwards he bathed in the river along with everybody else, dressed, packed his hammock and Basha kit and prepared to set off. Everything seemed easier this time round. The rucksack full of foodstuff that Kid had been put in charge of felt lighter, the mud seemed easier and the breaks seemed to come more frequently.

'Are you all right?' people kept asking, but they needn't have worried. Despite his expectations, Kid was beginning to enjoy himself. None of his research on Belize had prepared him for how beautiful it would be, nor how good it would feel to be so far away from cars, roads, pavements, shops, office blocks and all other signs of civilisation, including even burger bars. Snow walked in front of him, and she was beginning to feel like a friend. She didn't fuss over him like everybody else, but she did what no one else thought to do – which was fill him in on their project.

'We're going to build a bunkhouse for forest rangers up at Rio Blanco, on the Guatemalan border,' she said, 'so that the whole region can be patrolled to keep *xateros* at bay. Some of us will live there in our base camp, and do the building work, but the rest of us will spend our time trekking along the border, cutting a path and hanging up notices warning that this is a protected region, not to be entered without permission.'

'And you really think that dangerous, cut-throat bandits are going to bother with a notice like that?' Kid said, thinking of some of the villains he'd known back at home, and what they'd have made of it.

Snow shrugged. 'At least they won't be able to claim that they didn't know where the boundary was when the rangers catch them,' she said. 'But something's got to be done because they're moving through the forest, stripping it of everything from the plants on the forest floor – which end up in florist shop windows, would you believe – to monkeys, scarlet macaws and the last few jaguars to still live and breed out here in the wild.'

Kid's mind drifted off. It was interesting at first, but not when Snow went on and on. She was harping on now about decisions people would have to make about which team to join. Kid really didn't care. Nothing really mattered after Gold Mine, he reckoned, when he'd fall into his father's arms and these gap-year volunteers and their poxy project would become a thing of the past.

Lunch was taken beside a shallow stream where everybody tipped water over their heads and re-filled their bottles. It was good to lie in the shade eating tinned fish mashed up with baked beans, followed by peanuts and custard-cream biscuits. Someone took a photograph of a blue morpho butterfly, its wings glistening like jewelled enamel. Someone else found what they called 'this really cool bug' and everybody clustered round.

Kid didn't care about the bugs and butterflies. All he cared about was getting to Gold Mine. He thought of little else. The afternoon was dominated by mud, but it didn't distract his thoughts one iota. Kid hauled his mud-clogged boots across a stream, stumbled along a sunlit track, crossed the stream again, as it looped back on itself, and came out into the open to find himself standing on the edge of an enormous clearing.

This was it, apparently. Gold Mine, at last.

Everybody started cheering. Around the clearing grew the tallest trees Kid had ever seen. Their roots alone looked taller than a man, their trunks shone in the sunlight like silver, and they rose in massive columns to be crowned with foliage, like kings of the forest.

These were ceiba trees, Jez said. Holy trees, symbolising life itself. And Kid could quite see why. He started walking across the clearing. Beyond it stood a range of high green hills, but the clearing itself was anything but green – razed to sand and gravel by the mining company, which had rights here in this forest, according to Jez, that no amount of protection could legally prevent.

Kid passed great hulking lumps of machinery parked beside a tarpaulin camp where the miners lived. A table had been set up in front of the tarpaulins and on it were a clutter of things from another world – coffee cups, a bag of sugar, a portable radio covered in fine dust, somebody's knickers, a battered old paperback, somebody else's old socks.

A couple of miners sat at a bench in front of the table. It was evening now, the sun setting and their working day over. Someone in the background was cooking over a double-burner gas stove. Someone else was lying on a bunk bed behind a tarpaulin. All of them stared with undisguised curiosity as their visitors approached.

Jez went up to them and started talking in a mixture of Spanish and English. It was obvious that they knew each other. Even the miners' dog jumped round Jez's feet as if he was an old friend. Kid wondered if he did this all the time – trekked gap-year volunteers out here for projects in the forest. What a life, he thought. It certainly beat working in a burger bar.

Leaving Jez deep in conversation about pony trains and transporting equipment over the hills, Candy led the others down to the river to take off their boots and bathe their feet. The sky was darkening by now, and the moon rising above the tall green hills. Everybody looked up at it, marvelling at how huge it seemed, and how clear too. Some of them went off to find suitable trees for stringing up hammocks, but Kid returned to the camp where Jez seemed to have disappeared and the miners were sitting round their table eating supper.

They all looked up as Kid approached. Nervously he cleared his throat, sensing what the answer was likely to be before he even asked it. 'I'm looking for a man called Marcus Aurelius Cato,' he said. 'You don't know him, do you?'

The men stared blankly. A couple of them shook their heads. Kid pulled out his father's photograph as if to double-check.

'This isn't the owner of your mine, is it?' he said.

'El propietario de esta mina no es Kriol, como este hombre. Es Americano,' one of the miners said.

'Not a Creole, like this man,' translated another – though it wasn't necessary; Kid had got the general drift.

He went and sat with his back against a ceiba tree. So at least he knew that his father was a Creole now. Not that he was ever likely to need that particular piece of information. For, when it came to finding his father, he would always draw a blank. This thing was too big for him. He never should have taken it on.

Supper appeared, and Kid ate along with everybody else, though he didn't taste a thing. His mind was somewhere else. All this while, he'd been imagining arriving in Gold Mine and travelling no further. But his time with these gap-year volunteers wasn't over yet. He was stuck with them for a few more days.

Jez started talking about what they'd be facing tomorrow and, realising he'd be facing it as well, Kid started listening in. The worst of it all was going to be three steep, green, jungle-clad hills which they'd have to get over in order to reach their base camp on the other side.

'It's going to be a long day,' Jez warned them all.

'And a hot one,' Candy added. 'Which is why we need to be off at first light while the air's still cool.'

That night Kid lay awake, nursing his disappointed hopes. But morning, when it came, was beautiful, mist rising from the forest like an unravelling skein of silk and the first blush of gold breaking in the sky. Kid was up first, his Basha kit all packed up before anyone else awoke.

The group, when it set off, was swollen to include a pony train carrying building equipment, and a small contingent of soldiers which appeared out of nowhere, seemingly, and would be with them, Jez explained, from now on. A shiver ran through the group as they started off all together. The soldiers carried sub-machine guns slung over their shoulders. Their leader was a massive man who looked like Rambo, only black. His name was Hubert and he led the way with a ferocious-looking machete, cutting a path for them to follow as they left the clearing and headed uphill.

What were they in for? What lay ahead? Kid looked up a wall of green with no apparent end in sight. All around him people were looking up it too, their faces grim. The pony train went up first because it was fastest. It was followed by the soldiers with their machetes, and then the rest of them trudged along behind, a grim realisation dawning on them of what exactly they were in for.

A few people, determined to prove how tough they were, tried rushing ahead with the soldiers. And a few trailed behind, moaning at every step. But Kid steered a middle course between the two groups. No way was he going to show off like Hal and a big boy called Wallace and that joker, Fritz, who was already complaining that his shoes were rubbing, but refused to stop to find out why. But then no way was he grumbling either, like the rest of them.

Even so, Kid was relieved every time Jez or Candy called for a break. It took two breaks, an hour apart, to reach the top of the hill, then another hour's walking to come down the other side to the river. Jez told them they'd done fantastically well, but none of them were listening. They were too busy filling their hats with water which they then slammed on to their heads, filling their bottles, even lying down and letting the river flow over them.

For the first time since discovering that his father wasn't going to be at Gold Mine, Kid felt his spirits rise. People slapped him on the back as if he was one of them and not a stranger. He'd been through what they had, and they no longer treated him as if he'd come from another planet. And perhaps they weren't so different from him in return. Maybe they weren't just boring do-good geeks.

All around Kid, people lay about in a state of collapse. Nobody wanted to move, not even the soldiers. But the day was hot by now, the sun was high in the sky and according to Jez they still had a long way to go.

'The next hill will be easier,' he said.

'But de hill after dat,' Hubert said, 'maan, he's gonna be a killah.'

Kid struggled back into his rucksack. No matter how refreshed he felt, after a few minutes up the next hill, his time in the river might never have been. The air was so close that Kid felt physically crushed by it. Sweat poured off him in steady streams. Even walking in the shade didn't ease things.

Kid's back ached from the weight he was carrying. His legs felt like buckling and there was the terrible knowledge, courtesy of a grinning Hubert, that the third hill was going to be the worst.

And it was too. Hubert was right. Kid thought the second hill was difficult, but the third was cunning as well as steep. The third played games with them.

Every time they thought they'd made it to the top, there was always another incline waiting hidden up ahead. And when they thought they'd started down the other side, suddenly they'd find themselves heading back up again.

Hardly surprisingly, after hours of trekking, people started cracking. They'd had enough. Jack-the-Goth turned white with breathlessness. Star Wars Al panicked and said he was going to pass out. A couple of soft-skinned girls called Laydee and Tilda ended up in tears. Fritz's jokes dried up. A lad called Benji who'd been going on the entire trip about how much he loved snakes, saw one and nearly died of shock. Another lad called Jim said he wanted to go home. Later, he said he hadn't meant it, but he'd sounded as if he meant it to Kid.

Determinedly, he refused to complain however bad he felt. Some people were demanding rests every hundred yards or so, and a couple turned nasty when Jez refused to let them be carried by the ponies. But Kid wasn't one of those, and neither, he noticed, was that sulky boy, Hal. He kept his feelings to himself and never grumbled however hard things became.

Kid was impressed. 'How far now?' people kept asking. But a few of them, like Hal, just pressed on.

'Nearly there,' Jez kept saying. 'Another hour or so, and we should be down the other side.' Then, 'An hour and we'll be bathing in the Rio Blanco,' then, 'At the next break we'll be in the Rio Blanco,' then, 'I can nearly see it. Come on.'

Jez's words were meant to encourage, but those last few minutes scrambling down the hill were as difficult as anything they'd done all day. People plunged down through the trees, telling themselves that the worst was over. But that didn't stop them stumbling and falling, and getting down to the Rio Blanco seemed to take for ever.

Finally, tired as they'd never been tired in their lives, the entire group stumbled into the river where they bathed, refilled their bottles and drank long and deep. This was it at last. They had arrived. Now, they demanded to know, where was their camp?

Jez looked at Candy. Candy looked at Hubert. Hubert laughed and pointed up the next hill, which rose directly from the river. Everybody groaned. He had to be joking, they said.

He was, too. The camp turned out to be a mere five minutes' walk away, not heading uphill but following the river. In Kid's eyes, though, those were the longest five minutes of all. Once he failed to stoop low enough and a branch almost knocked him out. Then he missed his footing and was all-but catapulted into the water. Then he was so tired that he almost fell asleep on his feet and simply walked off among the trees.

Finally, though, the soldiers cut a path to an area of forest set above a shingly beach, where Candy threw down her rucksack and Jez said, 'Here we are.'

Everybody looked around. 'Here we are *where*?' said Fritz, speaking for the whole group.

'At our camp,' said Jez.

'What camp?' said Fritz.

'The one we trained you for that week at Gallon Jug,' said Jez. '*The one you're going to build.*'

PART FOUR
CHIQUIBUL FOREST

13

SETTING UP CAMP

The first thing Kid did was fling himself into the clear waters of the Rio Blanco to cool off. Then, aware that darkness would fall soon, he strung up his hammock. All round him, everybody else was doing the same, going through what might look like their usual end-of-the-day routine, but this was different. You could see how shocked and, in some cases, angry they were. There was nobody except for Fritz who could actually see the funny side of things. And there was only the smallest handful, including Hal and the big lad, Wallace, who looked as if they just might rise to the challenge. Everybody else, even Snow, looked utterly defeated.

While they were putting up their hammocks, Hubert flung together a bed of his own made out of palm fronds and saplings hacked down with his machete, then built a fire for supper and cooked a meal for everyone including the pony train men. It was a basic meal, nothing fancy, just rice and beans, but he threw in great dollops of a Belizean sauce called Marie Sharpe's, proving himself to be a regular Rambo in the kitchen too.

After supper, Jez made a speech. He knew how tired everybody was, but there were things he needed to say before they went to bed. Firstly they'd done brilliantly to get here without casualties and hold-ups, especially carrying all that weight. And secondly he wanted them to understand why it was good for them to build their camp from scratch.

Kid's mind drifted off. It wasn't *his* camp Jez was talking about. Tomorrow he'd be out of here. That's what Jez had said. Now that all the equipment had been ferried in, one of the leaders would lead him back to civilisation.

Candy was speaking now about the worthiness of the project ahead of them and the need to make decisions about which teams they wanted to join. Kid was glad he wouldn't have to make those sorts of decisions. He could see the lines of friendship forming already. Wallace, Jim and Joanne seemed to have bonded together, as had Snow and Fritz, Laydee and Tilda, Jack-the-Goth, Star Wars Al, Benji and a whole crowd of people whose names he didn't know.

Kid left them talking among themselves, and went to bed, easing himself into his hammock and waiting to fall asleep. Finally the others came too, the bobbing of their head-torches casting them in a jerky, almost silent movie light as they snuggled down their sleeping bags and tucked their mosquito nets around them. One by one, lights went out and the camp fell quiet save for Fritz, who was always singing to himself and even did it now as he fell asleep.

In the end, though, even he fell silent and only the soldiers remained awake, sitting over their fire talking to each other. Kid's hammock wasn't far from them, and he could hear what they were saying. As far as they were concerned, these British kids were crazy. Their projects were going to be impossible to complete in the time allocated, they weren't going to be able to cope with the heat and they didn't know what they were in for in a forest like this, full of jaguars, snakes and even the occasional evil spirit.

None of the soldiers, except for Hubert, ever wanted to be called up for jungle duty. The word was that there were *brujos* out here. But, worse still, some forest spirit called the *Duende* was meant to be found in these remote parts and some soldiers even reckoned that they'd seen another one called the *xtabay*.

'Wha' dese kids doin'?' one of them asked. 'We

heah bikaaz we in da army, an we gat no choice. But dey gat choice, for Krise sake. An' still dey heah. Wha' de matter wi dem?'

Next morning, Kid found out that Hubert would be the one trekking out with him, depriving everybody else of his cooking skills, not to say anything of his sense of humour and his vigour with a machete. Feeling decidedly guilty, Kid packed up his hammock ready to leave. Everybody was getting ready for a busy day ahead and he found himself almost wishing that he could stay and help. It felt the least he could do after all they'd already been through together as a group. For a few short days, these people had become like Kid's family. They'd given him something, and he wanted to give something back.

When Kid volunteered to stay for a couple of days until the camp was built, though, he surprised himself as much as anybody else. For a moment, Jez and Candy stared at him as if they didn't know what to say. Then Jez said, 'We could do with spare hands. You have to admit that,' and Candy agreed.

Suddenly Kid was in, wondering what he'd let himself in for. He was equipped with a machete and sent off to clear undergrowth, minding what he touched and keeping an eye out for snakes.

It was a long, hard day and Kid had plenty of

opportunities to regret his decision. By the end of it, however, he was pleased that he'd stayed, and everybody else seemed pleased as well. They'd worked flat out, clearing ground, cutting down branches to make the main frame of the kitchen, digging loos and constructing a food store.

Before supper, they went down to the river to wash, lark about and unwind from their labours. Then, after supper, they sat round on upturned logs and bedrolls and discussed which projects they might sign up for when it came time to choose.

Kid thought that if he'd been staying no way would he have signed up to work in the same team as Hal. All day long, Hal had been putting him down as if the only person who could do a thing properly was him. Kid glanced across at Hal now, and Hal gave him a look as if to say *Who d'you think you're staring at?* He was sitting next to Snow, who'd moved on from talking about teams to sharing what had brought her to Belize.

'My father used to work in Amsterdam,' she said. 'Our family lived by a canal. From our roof garden we could see spires and roof tops right across the city, and outside our front door was a market where people bought clothes, antiques and jewellery from across the world. That's when I first got a taste for travelling. I remember a stall selling Indonesian puppets in brightly embroidered costumes. I thought they were the most beautiful things I'd ever seen and I dreamt of going there one day. But then the next stallholder along brought in a scarlet macaw, and it was even more beautiful. I asked where it came from and the stallholder said Belize. I asked where that was. He told me to go and look it up.'

And so Snow had. And, after that, it had been Belize she'd dreamt of, though never thinking she'd end up here. Not long afterwards her parents had separated, which had meant the end of the house on the canal and definitely the end of the scarlet macaw. There had been arguments about who Snow should live with, and she'd ended up with her grandmother in England. Not that it stopped the arguments, because then her parents had started on about what she should be studying and what career she'd choose. Each had their own ideas, but neither asked her.

'So I decided to choose nothing and go on a gap-year trip instead,' said Snow, 'and the only trip I could sign up for at this late stage was this one. I was terrified of whether I was doing the right thing. At the airport, do you remember? You too, Kid, you were there as well.'

Kid stared at Snow as if she had to be talking about someone else. 'Who? Me? What?' he said.

'You don't remember, do you?' Snow said.

Kid said he didn't have a clue what she was on about. Snow laughed and said she was on about the automatic check-in machine at Heathrow Airport. 'You kept sticking your passport in upside-down,' she said. 'Remember? I thought I was nervous, but you were a real mess.'

Kid remembered what a fool he'd felt. He also just about remembered the blonde girl who had helped him, whom he'd seen later buying chocolates and again on the plane.

'That was *you*?' he said.

Snow laughed and said yes. It was a small world, she said. It had been niggling away at her for ages that she'd seen Kid before and suddenly today she'd remembered when.

'Life's full of coincidences,' she said. 'If that's what they are. We even travelled out together on the same plane.'

14

KID'S CHOICE

Next day, Hal made his presence felt as well. Whether Kid was helping dig steps down to the river, clear an emergency area at the top of the hill for a helicopter landing pad, construct the kitchen area, or help thatch its roof, Hal always knew a better way of doing it.

Just because Kid was a city boy, he seemed to think he was incapable. Kid almost wished he hadn't volunteered to stay. Hal might know how to repair barns and drive tractors, but that didn't give him the right to push people around.

'Hal's doing my head in,' Kid complained over lunch.

'You mustn't take it personally. He's just trying to be helpful. He's like that with everyone,' Snow said.

Kid told himself that she was right and just because he was a city boy and Hal a pig-headed country bumpkin, there was no reason why they couldn't get on. They had things in common, after all. They were both hard workers. Both liked getting stuck into things. Both wanted to do things well.

But both of them were impatient too, and when Hal made mistakes – as sometimes even he did – Kid never missed the chance to have a dig. And when Kid needed help, Hal would always make some passing jibe.

It took three days to build the camp and by the time it was finished Kid was ready to leave. The whole group went on a tour to admire what they'd achieved, but the greatest achievement for him wasn't the kitchen, or the flashy toilets – complete, in the boys' case, with a nifty target-practice device involving string and a tipping tin can – or the food store, sitting-room area or private chill-out place. It was surviving Hal.

That night – Kid's last – he was on supper duty, drawing on skills honed in Jet's Burger Joint to cook spam-burgers that went down a treat. All day long, he'd been counting the hours until he made his exit. But now, looking round at everybody, Kid wondered how he was going to say goodbye. Usually people came and went in his life and had little effect on him. But something special had happened here. These boring, rich-kid, do-gooders, as he'd once thought of them, had really proved themselves. For a few short days, they'd become Kid's friends.

After supper, people chose their projects. A list of teams went up and a strange atmosphere settled over the camp. Tomorrow it wasn't just Kid who'd be going his separate way, but half the group, heading off into the forest to start their boundary-marking work.

Their time together as one big group was nearly over, and everybody felt it. Kid looked round at them all. Wallace, Joanne, Snow, Hal, Fritz, Jack-the-Goth and Star Wars Al were among those who'd chosen the bunkhouse building team, and Laydee, Tilda, Jim and Benji among those who'd chosen to be boundary cutters. But they were all together for one last time, playing cards, laughing at each other's jokes, singing along with Fritz's silly songs and even sharing cigarettes – some of them using the excuse that they were only smoking to keep the mosquitoes at bay.

All around them stood the forest, alive with sound. Howler monkeys roared in the distance on their nightly journey across the forest canopy, cicadas whistled in the trees overhead and tree frogs croaked and whirred. Kid heard soldiers talking to each other in Kriol, and people trying to learn off them, repeating phrases and laughing at each other when they didn't get them right. The soldiers weren't just soldiers any more. They were Pablo, Renaldo, Myron, Gonzalo, Philip, Pedro and, of course, Hubert. Only a few days ago they'd been strangers – grim-looking men in camouflage, shouldering sub-machine guns. But now they were well on their way to becoming everybody's friends.

Leaving here was going to be really weird, Kid thought. In just a few short days he'd got used to living in the trees. *In the trees.* He liked that phrase. More than *bak-a-bush,* or *jungle* or even *forest,* it seemed to really mean something. To speak for a way of life that Kid would always remember with affection.

Like everybody else, he hung back that night instead of heading off to bed, unwilling for their precious time together to end. People started telling stories, and the soldiers joined in. The *xtabay* came up again – an evil witch-woman who Hubert swore blind he'd once come across hiding in the buttressed trunk of a ceiba tree, singing her song of seduction and he'd had to flee for his life.

'Dat's nothing,' said one of the other soldiers, Myron. 'If de *brujo* get you, you as good as dead. If de *xtabay* get you, you *is* dead. But if de *Duende* get you, you end up pleadin' fi death.'

Everybody wanted to know more. Who was the

Duende, they all asked. Myron explained that the *Duende* had the appearance of a wizened little old man, but really he was the guardian of the forest. To his friends, Myron said, he had it in him to be a friend too. But to anybody who harmed his beloved forest, be they the scariest *xatero* or the humblest gap-year volunteer, his wrath was terrible. In fact, being caught by him was worse than death.

'Blood an' death,' said Myron, rolling his eyes. 'Blood an' death, deep down an' dark. An' not jus' any death. Ai is talkin' *soul-death*.'

Everybody shivered when Myron said that. Kid remembered the little man he'd encountered when he'd been leaving Night Falls Lodge – the one whose every word of good advice he'd totally ignored. He hoped he hadn't been the *Duende* – not that he really believed in that sort of thing, of course.

People started talking about ways in which the forest was already being harmed. The gold mine had a mention, and so did the sorts of logging companies that were banned in Chiquibul. Hubert reckoned you could always tell a forest once it had been logged. Even after it had grown up again, there was a difference in the quality of light. A difference in the smell. A difference even in the sounds it made.

'Forests are like lungs,' Hubert said. 'Dey breathe life into us and mek us one. Heah we are from worlds apart and, thanks to de forest, we're sharing one life. Where we come from doesn't matter any more, or what we once were in de past. It's what we are now dat matters, here in de trees. It's what we do and what we mek of ourselves.'

Kid went to bed that night, Hubert's words ringing in his head, feeling as if leaving tomorrow would be a betrayal.

But these aren't my trees, he reminded himself. This isn't what I signed up to – it's not my cause. It's *their* cause – Snow's and Fritz's and everybody else's. And the cause of their organisation, Wide-World Treks. And the soldiers' cause, because this is their country. It's the Belizean people's cause, and their brand-new government. It's even the *Duende's* cause. *But it's not mine.*

Kid slept badly that night. Next morning he awoke to find half the group's hammocks packed away and the boundary cutters ready to depart. It was only first light, but already the camp was buzzing. Down in the kitchen area, breakfasts were being served and in the sitting-room area Candy and Doc Rose were going through their equipment list making sure they had everything they needed for a long trek.

Kid started making garbled farewells in a panic, afraid of people leaving before he had the chance to work his way round them all. Before he'd gone very far, however, Jez drew him to one side.

'I want a word with you,' he said.

Kid wondered what he'd done. Jez said he had an offer to make. His expression was grave.

'I don't know what you're going to think about this,' Jez said, 'and it's certainly not usual, believe me. But then your turning up out of the blue hasn't been usual either, and we've been talking about it and we'd like you to stay. The choice is yours, of course. Hubert's all lined up to trek you out. But we could do with another worker, truth to tell, and you're not just any worker – you work damn hard. And, apart from that, you've become a mate. I'm not just speaking for us leaders here. I'm speaking for everyone. So *what do you think*?'

What did Kid think? He looked round to find everybody listening in. 'You mean . . . you want . . . you're asking me . . . you're offering for me to become a proper signed-up volunteer?' he said, struggling for words like a foreigner who didn't understand the language.

Everybody grinned. 'No pressure – but could you decide in the next five minutes?' Candy called out.

Kid burst out laughing. A few days ago he'd have said no way. In fact, even last night he'd have still said no way, not months in the jungle with a gang of gap-year volunteers.

But now Kid thought *why not?* What else was he going to do with his time here in Belize? What plan had he made? What itinerary had he drawn up? His search for his father had drawn a blank, and what else had he got?

By this time the whole group had stopped what they were doing and were waiting for an answer. Everyone was beaming except for Hal, and even he was trying his best. Kid looked round at them all. They were giving him a chance – but it wasn't only them, was it? The forest was giving him a chance as well. And Belize was giving him a chance. Even the trees were giving him a chance to live the way that Hubert had said last night, where it didn't matter where you came from, or what had happened in your past. All that mattered was right here and now.

'Why not?' Kid said at last, knowing he'd be a fool to let this pass him by. 'What have I got to lose? Okay, everybody. Cheers for that – *I'll stay.*'

15

WILD PECCARIES

It went down well, but there was no time for Kid to savour his moment of glory, everybody whooping and whistling their approval, because he had a team to choose – and he had to do it quickly, before the boundary cutters set off.

Kid tried to focus his mind. One thing was for sure – whichever team he chose, life from now on was going to be challenging. He looked across at the boundary cutters, gathered around their equipment ready for the off. They didn't include Hal, which had to be a bonus, and they did include Doc Rose, who was a reassuring figure to have around. But the bunkhouse builders had Cassie, who was every bit as experienced at being a medic on jungle expeditions. And Snow was in that team as well – and whatever was good enough for her was good enough for Kid.

He made his choice. Even though it meant work-ing in the same team as Hal, he chose to spend the next two months of his life in the bunkhouse-build-ing team. It was sad, though, to see the others go. They headed off between the trees, weighed down with equipment, promising to make radio contact when they reached their first night's destination. After they'd gone, the camp looked empty and sounded strangely flat. Someone said the obvious – that the boundary cutters were going to be missed. But they were missed already and they'd only just left.

Jez tried to cheer things up, saying that it would only be a couple of weeks before they'd see each other again, and runners would be going back and forth anyway, ferrying provisions. Besides, the two teams would be meeting up for a break in the mid-dle of their projects at the ruined Mayan city of Caracol, deep in the heart of the jungle. It would be their treat for working hard, he said, their chance to have a little holiday. Caracol was amazing. It was something they simply had to see. They'd all have a party there, and if anybody felt they'd chosen the wrong team, that would be their chance to swap projects.

'In the meantime, though,' Jez said, 'the chance we're facing is to prove ourselves. There's a bunkhouse waiting to be built . . .'

The first day was spent doing nothing but hauling equipment. Everybody worked flat out to bring things up from the river where the pony train had left them and deposit them on the hilltop above the camp, where the bunkhouse would be built. Before they started, however, Jez led them up to see for themselves the problems the forest faced.

They stood on a bare, sun-baked hilltop with miles of green forest rolling away from them and not a road in view, or any sign of habitation. People marvelled that the forest was so vast, and so unbroken too. But then Jez led them to the other side of the hill, where the view was still green, but it was a completely different sort of green.

Kid was the one who said it. 'What's that?' he said, pointing to an area of low undergrowth on the hill opposite theirs, with not a tree in sight, just scrubby little bushes and patches of dry ground.

'*That*, as you put it, is the problem,' Jez replied. 'That's why we're here. Down there in the valley beneath us is the Belizean border and that scrubland is coming its way. In fact it's already over the border in some places. Like this hilltop where we're standing now. How do you think it came to be so bare? You see those great old ceiba trees behind us? Well, this time next year, they won't be here. Unless this border country is guarded, they'll all be gone.'

'I'm not a man for preaching,' Jez had said, 'but this sermon preaches itself. You can see the problem. People talk about the destruction of rain forests. Well, now you've seen it with your own eyes. *There it is.*'

Kid turned away. He didn't want to look. People were asking why, and how, and Jez was trying to explain about the scale of poverty that drove people over the border to strip a forest like this. But Kid didn't want to hear. All around him, the smell of trees rose from the ground, earthy, dank and spicy, just the way he'd smelt it that first day at the airport. He'd heard a voice that day, which he'd thought was calling out a welcome.

But really it had been calling out for help.

For the rest of the day, Kid worked like a man possessed. The choice he'd made this morning over breakfast had been to suit himself. He'd been latching on to someone else's cause – but now, he realised, it was his cause too.

Only when a downpour put a temporary end to work did Kid stop, huddling with the others under a hastily constructed tarpaulin. The rain was like steel rods, making it physically impossible to carry on working.

But the sun quickly reappeared afterwards, and a

chorus of birds burst into life, accompanied by a rhythm section of raindrops dripping from leaf to leaf. All sorts of insects came out too, as if rejuvenated, and started drying their wings. The rain had certainly flushed them out – bugs of every colour, size and shape, some bright and beautiful and some looking distinctly hostile.

Stories started doing the rounds about insects that needed to be looked out for. The subject of bot flies came up, and people started examining themselves anxiously for eggs under their skin. No one found any, but the idea of flies hatching out and feeding on their flesh had them all shuddering. This was no garden that they were in, no matter how beautiful it might be. This was no playground. From the mighty jaguar to the tiniest insect they were surrounded by danger if they didn't take care.

This message was hammered home forcefully at the end of the day. Work had finished for the night and the team was walking down the trail in single file, heading back to camp. Hal was towards the front of the file, with Kid directly behind him, dreaming of the long cool swim he intended to take in the Rio Blanco. Suddenly a hint of something musky came wafting his way. He looked up, and other people did as well. They took a few more steps only for it to grow more pungent.

Finally everybody at the front of the file stopped in their tracks. What was that smell? They couldn't see anything, but the smell was growing stronger all the time and a clicking noise had started up as well.

At the back of the file, but plain for everyone to hear, Jez said the single word *peccary*. Immediately, everybody started backing up the track. People wanted to get out of reach, and they wanted to do it quickly. Jez told them to stay calm but they didn't listen, and the soldiers weren't much of an example. With their experience of the jungle, Kid would have thought a few wild animals in the undergrowth wouldn't have bothered them. But the soldiers were backing up as fast as anybody else.

Kid peered between the trees. The word *peccary* meant nothing to him and he was curious to see what all the fuss was about. At first he couldn't see anything, but then – half-camouflaged by dappled sunlight – he became aware of a face looking back at him. It was solid, snouted, and its tiny piggy eyes fixed on Kid in a way that even he could tell meant trouble.

Kid started backing away as well, but then the clicking started on the far side of the track and all hell broke out amongst the team. Kid caught a glimpse of a second peccary staring in bewilderment at the first British teenagers it had ever seen, as if trying to make up its mind whether to kill them or not.

And that was when Hal decided to attack.

People talked about it afterwards for days. Jez yelled at Hal to get back, but Hal thwacked through the undergrowth with his machete, making weird noises that might startle squirrels back home in Shropshire, but definitely didn't impress Belizean peccaries. Immediately the peccaries started making noises back. These should have been enough to stop Hal in his tracks, but he upped his own noise and carried on, brandishing his machete.

After that, everything happened in a matter of seconds. The peccaries moved forward. So did both Jez and Hubert, trying to put themselves between the peccaries and Hal. But they weren't close enough – and Kid was. Acting on pure instinct, he grabbed Hal, wrested the machete out of his hand and dragged him away. If he hadn't moved so quickly, Hal could have ended up gored to death.

Not that Hal saw it like that. He was almost as furious with Kid as Jez was with him.

'You were unbelievable!' Jez shouted at him when they'd somehow got themselves down the hill in one piece and were back in camp. 'You could have got someone killed – and I'm not just talking about yourself. And after all that jungle training at Gallon

Jug! You know how dangerous peccaries can be, especially when aroused. And yet still you had to act the little hero, didn't you! *What got into you?*'

Hal didn't have a word to say in his defence. Later, however, he took it all out on Kid.

'You have to stand up to creatures in the wild,' he said. 'Show them who's master. I knew exactly what I was doing. Those peccaries would have fled if you hadn't snatched my machete. Things went pear-shaped because of you.'

It was the end of any even mild pretence that Kid and Hal could be friends. Everybody rushed to Kid's defence, which meant that, on top of everything else, Hal blamed Kid for the team turning against him.

After that, the atmosphere was as sour as vinegar. Hal's pride was wounded, but he didn't see it like that. Kid was a troublemaker, he said. And he was flaky under fire. Right from the moment he'd first set eyes on him, Hal had known he couldn't be trusted. Nothing Kid could do now would ever change his mind.

16

KID'S BIRTHDAY

Unable to put things right, Kid put all his energy into the project instead, reminding himself that this was why he was here – not to get along with Hal but to do a job that mattered and do it well. Everything he attacked was accomplished with a vigour that would have amazed his teachers back at school in England, and even astonished Burger-Bar Jet.

After a couple of weeks not even Hal could have taught Kid anything about how to build and which tools to use. But Kid's body was beginning to pay a high price. His hands were blistered from sawing, hammering, screwing and chiselling from morning to night, and every evening his arms, legs and face were covered with fresh insect bites.

People started running sweepstakes for who would have the most. Mosquito bites were easy to count, but the tiny, highly itchy blood blisters left behind by the sand flies that everybody called 'fuck-you flies' seemed as numerous as the stars in the sky.

Kid's legs in particular were covered with them. He'd be down in the river at the end of the day, in the water to stop himself scratching, unwilling to get out, dreaming of hot showers, fluffy towels, ice-cold Belikin beers and legs that didn't itch. Fritz would be there too, bathing his manky feet which were progressively getting worse because he didn't dry them properly and his jungle boots didn't fit.

Cassie, in her role as medic, would try to offer help, but Fritz wouldn't let her anywhere near him. He hated fuss, he said. He'd sort it out. His feet were fine and so was he.

'Some people might need pampering, but not a boy like me. I've been brought up tough.'

Cassie would stomp off moaning, 'Be it on your own head – or, in this case, feet.' But she wasn't alone. Everyone, these days, had taken to moaning. The first glow of achievement had worn thin and all over the camp grumbles were springing up and people beginning to fall out. It wasn't just Kid and Hal who couldn't get on. It was beginning to feel like all of them.

One night a particularly nasty row blew up out of Hubert killing a fer-de-lance with his machete.

Their numbers were swelled on that occasion by the boundary cutters who'd returned to camp for fresh provisions. The die-hard conservationists amongst them all, including Joanne, Sam and Laydee, were outraged at this loss to the world of an innocent snake. But others agreed with Hubert that there were no such things as innocent snakes, especially when it came to fer-de-lances, that not only were deadly but were famed for their aggressive natures.

Everybody took sides. One group reckoned that what Hubert had done was inexcusable, flying in the face of everything they were here to achieve. The other group argued that, if the fer-de-lance had had its way, nothing would be achieved because they'd all be dead.

'It's them or us,' they said.

Laydee argued that every creature – *every creature* – had the right to life. But Hal reckoned that, in the jungle, dog eat dog was the order of the day. And a sizeable number of the team agreed with him.

Jez, as leader, tried to steer a middle course. The right to life couldn't be denied, he said, and to kill a creature in the wild was a terrible thing. But the right to self-protection couldn't be denied either. You couldn't mess where fer-de-lances were concerned. Of all the snakes you were likely to come across in Belize, they were the only ones who could jump at you from three times their body length and kill you with their venom.

In the end, the argument turned bitter. People were tired, which was probably why, but they went to bed that night with words ringing in their ears that should never have been said. It was an unhappy end to a day that everyone had looked forward to because the whole group would be together again. To make matters worse, Cassie had finally managed to make a medical examination of Fritz, at Jez's insistence, and announced him to be on the verge of trench foot.

'It's three days in camp for you,' she'd said. 'Off your feet, if you please, and wearing no shoes or socks. You have to let the air get at your feet, and you're to stay out of the river. It's important to keep your feet dry.'

Gloom hung over the camp that night. Kid lay in his hammock feeling sorry for Fritz, but just as sorry for himself because tomorrow, unbeknown to anybody else, was his birthday and the way things were going, it didn't look as if it was going to be a particularly good one. Not that his birthdays ever were much good. But at least this one was being spent in a place he liked, amongst people he liked being with, if only they could be persuaded to get on with each other.

Kid awoke early next morning, determined to make the most of the occasion, no matter how anybody behaved. The boundary cutters went off with their provisions, seemingly unaware that there was anything special about the day, and the bunkhouse builders tramped up the hill to work.

At lunchtime, Kid pretended that his mess tin was full of birthday cake and his tin mug brimming with Belikin beer. Then, walking back down the hill at the end of the day, he imagined he was heading for his birthday party, all dressed up in brand-new kit.

When they reached the camp, he headed for his hammock, wanting time alone to savour his new age, which made him feel, for the first time, almost as old as the others. But, when he tried to extract himself from them, they weren't having it.

'Kid,' they said. 'You're not going anywhere until you've had a wash. In that river. *Now*. You stink. Do us a favour before we all pass out.'

Taken utterly by surprise, Kid found himself picked up and carried bodily into the Rio Blanco. He shouted and protested but it made no difference. Everybody was there, carrying him past his usual bathing place and round a long bend in the river to where the boundary cutters – *the boundary cutters, who were meant to have left this morning* – leapt back from something like guilty children.

What was going on here? Kid was dropped into the river. Shower gel was thrust into his hands by Joanne. The boundary cutters parted to reveal a weird-looking contraption which they had fixed to the overhanging branch of a tree. Kid stared up at one of the water-containers from the kitchen, which had been daubed with soot from the fire to blacken it. A series of tubes, forks and a sieve had been attached to it, and a rustic curtain made out of stitched-together black plastic bin-liners had been strung up in front of it.

'What the hell is that?' Kid said. 'I don't understand.'

Everybody laughed and said Kid didn't need to understand. All he needed was to get in.

'Get into *what?*' Kid said.

'Your birthday shower!' they shouted at him. 'The one you're always going on about, with proper running water. Remember?'

Of course Kid remembered. He burst out laughing. 'How did you know it was my birthday?' he said.

No one would own up, but later Kid found out that he'd mentioned it to Jez that first time by the river when he'd told him his life story. 'You mean I even told you that?' he said. 'You told me everything,' Jez said.

Everybody shouted at Kid to get his clothes off and get in. And he didn't need to be told again.

To an accompaniment of voices singing 'Happy Birthday to You', Kid stripped off and stepped into the shower for six long blissful minutes of sheer heaven before the hot water finally ran out. Maybe Joanne's shower gel wasn't quite as bubbly as Nadine's back in England, but then hers wouldn't have been bio-degradable.

Kid emerged when the last drop of water had finally run dry. His face was shining. His hair was squeaky-clean. Every bit of him was squeaky-clean, and the sight of Jez holding out to him the only remaining item that could possibly be on his wish list – an ice-cold Belikin beer – was almost more than he could bear.

'Where did you get that from?' he yelled.

'You're not going to believe this, so I don't know if I should tell you,' Jez said.

'Go on,' said Kid.

'It's a famous fact,' Jez said.

'What's a famous fact?'

'Belizean rivers run with Belikin beer.'

Kid laughed at that. So did everybody else. Jez said, 'You don't believe me . . .?' plunged down beneath the surface of the water and came up with a whole crate of Belikins.

Everybody yelled this time, not just Kid.

'How did you do that?' they wanted to know. 'Where did they come from? How did you smuggle them in without us knowing?'

But Jez never told them. It was his secret.

After that, they ate and drank, sang, danced and gambled wildly on a roulette table fashioned by Star Wars Al and Jack-the-Goth out of flattened tin cans. The gloom was lifted as if no disagreements had ever taken place. Someone got out a mouth organ. Someone else turned a couple of cans into bongo drums. Everybody danced.

Then Fritz got out a piece of paper, folded it flat and, in the light of his head-torch, sang a special song. It had started as a poem, he said, but he'd been working to turn it into a song ever since he'd known about Kid's birthday.

'It's dedicated to you all,' he said. 'But especially to Birthday Boy here. It's sort of about us all, and our life here in the forest, and our lives back at home, and our families and friends. I call it "Paradise".'

Everybody fell quiet and Fritz sang unaccompanied:

The birds and the bees and the fish in the seas
Couldn't have a better time than you and me.
Here together, they've been here for ever
Living in perfect peace.

In this garden of God, with our staff and our rod
We will roam and ramble and plod,
We are here to observe, to maintain and preserve
This most glorious garden of God.

Well, it came to me in a series of dreams,
That not everything is all it seems
My brother's disguises are all that he prizes
But they're gone when he puts them to sleep.

My sister's heart craves more for her part
Than anyone could ever give,
Too much to buy, with too little time,
Not enough life left to live.

Friends on the street, they call up to me
They've found a dead dog on the road
They laugh and they joke at this sad body broke,
Their duty to life they don't know.

Brothers and sisters, friends and neighbours,
All who choose to hear,
I've been away for a number of days
And must sing my song to you clear.

You may not like it, you may rebuke it,
You may throw it back in my face,
But truth must be told, be it ever so bold,
We're just gardeners of this place.

Earth is not ours for the taking,
Whatever our birthplace or breed,
It's only a mess we are making,
Only deeper will our digging lead.

We are on this planet, not of it,
Caretakers roaming free,
And whilst we can take what we want and have it,
Earth is not ours – nor shall ever be . . .

The last note trailed off and everybody sat in silence. The tune lingered in the air long after Fritz had stopped. When he finally looked up, there was a hint of tears in his eyes. Where was the joker now? Where was the writer of funny songs, who always had them all in fits of laughter? People said the song was amazing, but they only said that because they had to say something. The word amazing wasn't right at all.

Finally a few people started drifting off to bed, including Fritz, whose feet were bothering him, he said, and Jez, who said it would be work the same time as usual in the morning – they should bear that in mind if they decided to sit up until five o'clock mixing cocktails out of beer and Kool-Aid.

But the boundary cutters were greedy for any gossip that they'd so far missed, and there were plenty of people, including Kid, who were willing to stay up and fill them in on who fancied whom, who'd fallen out with whom and whether any *xateros* had been seen.

They sat up together until the questions all finally ran dry. Then they still sat up, unwilling for the night to end. Fritz's song had been amazing, Tilda said, trying to keep the conversation going. And so sad, when one thought about the poor guy's own background. She felt really sorry for him.

Why sorry? everybody wanted to know. And what background? What did Tilda mean?

Tilda lowered her voice. It had been there in the song, she said, in a tone of voice that couldn't help but give away how much she enjoyed gossiping. All that stuff about brothers and sisters, and having things thrown back in your face.

'Fritz is only here because his family hates him,' she said, 'and want to be rid of him. He's the oldest son, which means he's inherited loads of money, and his brothers and sisters are jealous of him. And a castle. He's inherited that too. And a title, would you believe. His real name's not Fritz, you know. It's

Clarence James William Oliver Something-hyphen-Something else, Lord of Dah-de-Dah – I can't remember what.'

If Tilda had said that Fritz was king of England, Kid couldn't have been more shocked. 'Fritz is a lord?' he said. 'A *lord*? How do you know that?'

'I picked it up during jungle training,' Tilda said.

There was more apparently, but Kid didn't want to hear it. Let Tilda gossip if she wanted, but he was heading off for bed. He'd heard enough.

Lying in his hammock, though, Kid couldn't sleep. Fritz was one of the lads. He was one of Kid's mates. He was a regular guy, like anybody else. He didn't act posh. He didn't even sound posh. He was just himself – a joker one minute, a real hard worker the next. Not some wet-eared lord who lived in a castle somewhere, but a down-to-earth guy who didn't even complain about his terrible feet.

Next day the boundary cutters set off again – this time for real – saying they'd meet up again at Caracol. After they'd gone, the bunkhouse builders dragged themselves up the hill to work, knowing that it was going to be difficult after a night of partying. They gave it their best shot though and, at the end of the day, Jez congratulated them.

'When I first met you lot,' he said, 'I didn't know what to make of you. But I'm really proud of you.

Time and again you've proved the critics wrong who think that gap-year projects aren't about hard work, and the people who go on them are only interested in having fun.'

Jack-the-Goth said that everything young people did these days always got put down. If they passed exams, he said, they were never as hard as in their parents' day. If they pierced their noses, they were thugs. And if they went on gap-year projects, however challenging, they were accused of bumming round the world, simply having a good time.

Fritz agreed. 'People think that only rich kids do things like this,' he said, 'because their parents pay for them. They don't want to hear about the challenges we face, not least in raising funds to get out here.'

Kid snorted at that. He couldn't help himself, but the others didn't seem to notice.

'I can't talk,' Snow confessed. 'My trip was paid for by my grandmother – but I do intend to pay her back.'

'My trip was funded by working in a laundry,' Joanne said, 'which I hated, by the way.'

'I wrote off for sponsorship,' said Wallace, 'and earned the rest working in a pub.'

Most of the others had done a mix of both, sponsorship and work. Apart from Snow, only Star Wars

Al had had the whole thing paid for him outright. But he said it was only because his brother had won money on the lottery.

Fritz said, 'No such luck for me. In order to get out here I had to work every school holiday for a year. In fact, I even worked on Christmas Day.'

Kid laughed at that. It wasn't a nice laugh – and this time people heard.

'What's eating you?' Fritz said.

Kid knew that he should stop, but couldn't do it. It had been a long, hard day and he didn't have the energy for self-restraint. Besides, what other people had worked to fund-raise for had come his way for free, and the conversation made him feel defensive.

'What's eating me?' he said, surprised by the force at which his words came out. 'I'll tell you what. *It's people who tell lies.*'

The group fell silent. Kid's words were so unexpected that for a moment no one knew what to say. Then Hal spoke up. 'What are you on about?' he demanded, as if he had some special role as Fritz's defender. 'Come on. Spit it out. That was a nasty thing you just said. Explain yourself.'

Kid sensed a trap, but couldn't step back. 'I'm on about Fritz being a lord,' he said, 'and owning a castle and being rich. He doesn't need to pretend he's like the rest of us, working on Christmas Day and things like that. He can drop the regular-guy crap. We all know the truth.'

Kid looked at Fritz when he said that, and Fritz flushed as if he'd been landed a punch. 'You're a liar,' Kid said. 'If you're rich you should have said. *A liar and a hypocrite.*'

His words echoed round the group. No one knew where to look. But then Snow spoke for all of them. Her face was flushed with anger and her voice was shaking.

'It doesn't matter *who* Fritz is,' she said. 'He doesn't have to say, and neither does anybody else. This is the jungle, for God's sake, the place where everybody is the same. Here it doesn't matter who any of us were back in our old lives. How *dare* you speak to Fritz like that? Who do you think you are?'

Kid felt everybody's eyes on him. He struggled to say something that would put things right, but the damage was done. People didn't want to know. One by one, they walked away.

'Well, you messed up there,' said Jez when no one else was left.

'You don't have to tell me that,' Kid replied.

Next day Fritz wouldn't look him in the eye. Kid wanted to say sorry but couldn't get near for Fritz's army of friends. Hal gloated openly, delighted at the turn events had taken. But Kid knew it wasn't Hal to blame. He'd done this to himself. If the whole team turned against him, it was only what he deserved.

It took Snow a couple of days to speak to him. Finally she came round, but there was an awkwardness between them after that. And Kid never got the chance to put things right with Fritz. A few days later, having continued to keep him off work, Cassie finally said enough was enough. She showed Fritz's feet to Jez, who agreed that she was right, and Fritz was informed that he'd have to go to hospital.

'What d'you mean, hospital?' he protested. 'There's nothing wrong with me, only my feet.'

'You won't have feet much longer if you don't get some medical attention,' Cassie said.

After that, things happened very quickly. An emergency air-ambulance flew in, which Fritz wasn't even allowed to walk to but had to be stretchered. Kid tried to get close enough to wish him luck, but couldn't make himself heard above everybody else. Cracking jokes to hide how much he cared, Fritz was lifted into the helicopter.

'See you later,' he called out.

But he knew he wouldn't. You could see it in his eyes.

17

JAGUAR

It came as a shock to see Fritz go, but then so did discovering that the outside world was only thirty minutes' flight away. That was how long it took to airlift him to hospital in Belize City. Maybe their camp in Rio Blanco was miles away from civilisation, but civilisation wasn't miles away from it.

The word came back via Jez's satellite phone that Fritz was being taken good care of in hospital, and Wide-World's field manager, Craig, from their base in San Ignacio, was with him. The situation was serious, but Fritz was in good hands.

Kid knew he shouldn't, and that it made no sense, but he felt to blame. Maybe Fritz had left because of his feet, but Kid couldn't help feeling as if he'd left because of him. For the next few days he worked like the furies to make up to the team for being one man short. But everyone was cool with him, and an air of gloom hung over the camp. Not even the unexpected sighting of a pair of scarlet macaws one morning could raise a cheer. Someone saw them. Someone else pointed. They all looked up. And that was it.

Work progressed slowly, and a string of rainy days spent labouring through mud didn't help. The soldiers grumbled that it wasn't the rainy season yet. Even Hubert, who could see the best in every situation, complained about the weather being all upside-down.

Some days work ground to a halt completely and people spent their time under the tarpaulin playing cards. But no sooner had Jez started talking about their falling behind their schedule, jeopardising the Caracol trip, than the rain clouds blew away and the sun came out to stay.

Work started motoring at last. The bunkhouse floor was finished off. Its walls went up. Work began on the frame to take the roof. People laboured until dark and were up again at dawn.

'If things stay on schedule, we'll be off in a week,' Jez said. Then, 'If they stay on course, it'll be a couple of days.' Then, after liaising with Candy on the satellite phone to find out where the boundary cutters were, 'That's it. *We're off tomorrow.*'

All bunkhouse building ended that day at lunch

165

time, and the afternoon was spent preparing for the trek. For the first time in weeks people would be leaving the confines of Rio Blanco, and excitement hung in the air. That night, everybody fell into their hammocks with their minds full of ruined cities, Mayan temples and the party they'd be having with their boundary-cutting friends.

A breeze blew through the forest that night, bringing with it a sense of change. Kid was awake early, eager to be off. It wasn't even light yet, but he got up for a pee, trying not to waken anybody, and started creeping through the camp. The breeze had blown itself out by now and, in the stillness of dawn, something moved in the kitchen area. Kid tried to see what it was, and realised it was a dog.

Kid forgot about peeing. The dog was in the kitchen area, rummaging for scraps. But, as everybody knew, there were no wild dogs in the forest and the nearest semi-domestic ones were over the hills in Gold Mine. Whose dog, then, was this? Kid drew in his breath. He couldn't see anyone but, just as he was about to take a step forward, a low whistle from behind him called the dog away.

Kid span round. In the first thin light of morning he could see the food store, its shelves packed with provisions. He could also see a figure standing between them, staring straight at the dog as it bounded towards him. He wore an old string vest, ragged jeans, a pair of battered-looking trainers and a baseball cap. He was as thin as a rake and clutching a sack which he'd been filling with food.

Kid let out a cry, and the figure saw him. He turned towards Kid and, in his free hand, Kid saw a gun. The two of them stared at each other. The moment was alive with possibilities. Kid could have shouted a warning across the camp. He could have launched a one-man attack. He could have aimed for getting back the food. He could have ducked, or dived or gone for the gun. Was it loaded, or was it just a threat? And what about the dog – would it attack?

For a moment Kid did nothing, though. For this was a *xatero*, wasn't it? One of the mighty *xateros* that they were being guarded against. And yet there was no difference between him and Kid. He was just a boy. A poor boy, living on his wits. And so was Kid. They were both the same. Both trying to get by. Both making the best of what came to hand.

When the *xatero* turned and fled, Kid let him go. A couple of the tins of food fell out of his sack, but he took the rest, melting with his dog into the forest, whistling to it as they both disappeared.

Later Kid was held to blame for the stolen food. He didn't want to admit what had taken place, but it was immediately obvious that half a shelf was empty. Hal said that, in Kid's shoes, he'd have chased that food all the way back to Guatemala. Jez said that losing it meant everybody would have less to eat. He was worried about the *xatero* coming back and bringing others too. Between them, he and Hubert decided that instead of leaving just a couple of soldiers to guard the camp, they'd leave them all and only Hubert would accompany the trek.

It wasn't exactly the best start to their holiday. With a sense of trepidation, they crossed the Rio Blanco and headed off into the jungle wondering what would happen while they were away and whether they'd be safe with three soldiers fewer to protect them. It was a long day's trek, first following the path of the river, then cutting through the jungle, then finally reaching another river, which fell in a series of tumbling pools to the place where they set up camp.

Here Jez talked to them for the first time about Caracol. It mightn't look like it, he said, but already they'd crossed the city boundary and tomorrow they'd be heading along one of seven great causeways leading to the city centre. This city was vast, he said. It went on for miles, which meant they weren't to think they'd arrive by tomorrow night. But when they *did* arrive, there'd be temples waiting for them, and mighty palaces, sweeping plazas and fabulous observatories charting the night skies.

'The Maya were a great people in their day,' Jez said. 'The wise ones of the ancient world. But now their glory days are over and only ruins remain.'

Everybody shivered. Joanne wondered if a similar fate would one day befall modern cities like London and New York. 'In a thousand years' time,' she said, 'will people discover our ruins and wonder what *we* were like?'

Next morning people awoke with a sense of anticipation, expecting Caracol to be within their grasp despite what Jez had said. But they walked for hours without sight of a single stone. The only excitement came from a troop of howler monkeys, who hurled twigs at their heads for coming too close.

That night, they camped close to another river. People went down to bathe, but returned with their legs covered with sand fly bites. No one wanted to go near to it after that but, just before turning in, Kid slipped down to fill his water bottles, and Snow joined him.

Night was falling, the last light leaching out between the trees and the river shining like a piece of polished ebony. Everything was still, as if the forest held its breath. Snow said something about hallowed ground. Kid said he didn't know what hallowed meant. Snow said it meant the sort of things that Fritz had sung about. The holiness of life. The garden of God.

The two of them stood in silence, looking at the river which was shining darkly now. Suddenly Kid became aware that something was slicing through those waters, long silvery lines running from what surely had to be a creature's head.

By Kid's side, Snow drew in her breath. She took Kid's hand and he too drew in his breath. The something rose up from the river, dripping with water, and padded ashore. Unheralded, terrifying but utterly beautiful – it was a jaguar.

A jaguar.

Kid moved his lips, but no sound came out. Even so, as if aware of having an audience, the jaguar turned its enormous head. Its twin eyes burned like black-hearted fires and, in a teasing parody of a yawn, the jaguar opened its cavern of a mouth revealing white fangs and a huge tongue.

Snow huddled against Kid's side, clutching his arm, her nails digging into his skin. But Kid didn't feel her. Her presence was forgotten. Everything about this jaguar's body was on a grand scale, starting with its coat, dappled with a pattern of dark rosettes. Its shoulders were huge and rippling with muscles. Its legs were as solid as tree trunks. Even its paws were huge.

Kid wondered why he wasn't quaking in his shoes. He should have been, he knew, but everything inside him felt icy calm. For the single, most electric moment of his life the jaguar stood watching him with its gold-black eyes.

Then, as if it had seen enough, it turned and stalked away.

18

CARACOL

The jaguar changed things – not just for Kid and Snow, but for the whole trek. It changed its outcome in unexpected ways. From that point onwards nothing was quite the same. The whole team was changed, and Hal more than the rest of them. He never quite got over the fact that Kid, not him, had seen that jaguar.

Kid was the hero of the hour. 'He was so calm,' Snow said. 'He was amazing. He made me feel so safe. He made me feel protected.'

Hal walked away. He didn't want to know. Everybody was envious, but not like him. Kid tried to make Snow stop, but the damage was already done.

From then on, Hal's nickname for Kid was Jaguar-Boy. He said it a couple of times over supper, then started up with it again as soon as they set off next day.

'Come on, Jaguar-Boy,' he said. 'Hurry up. Watch your step. Who's the hero now? You're holding everybody up.'

Kid told Hal to leave it off. But Hal carried on all day in similar vein. It was a hot day too, perfect for short tempers. Even by the jungle's standards the heat was remorseless. The jungle felt like an oven. Yesterday there'd been a bit of sky between the trees, but today they were impenetrable. The foliage created a dense wall on either side of them as they fought their way through. The canopy was heavy overhead, and the little bits of light that seeped through had a strange hardness about them.

And the jungle seemed more humid, too. Kid poured with sweat all day long. His legs, feet, shoulders, head, arms, eyes – everything – were soaked in sweat, and aching too. He started laughing but didn't know why. Jez said they hadn't far to go, but Kid didn't believe him. After all, this was the same Jez who'd billed this trek as a holiday – and look how right he'd been about that!

Other people started laughing too, as if they'd passed some sort of pain threshold and nothing mattered any more. When word came back from somewhere towards the front of the group that Jez was right, nobody at the back where Kid was believed it.

'What are you laughing at, Jaguar-Boy?' Hal said.

Kid laughed at him as well. How come he'd never noticed how funny Hal was before? He struggled on, dragging his feet, head down, not noticing the growing light until suddenly it burst in upon him and he found himself standing in a clearing carpeted by coarse grass.

Three tall trees grew right in the middle of the clearing, their roots protruding from a white stone wall. For some reason, Kid found that funny too. He laughed until he thought he'd burst. All around him people were whooping, cheering and throwing down their rucksacks, but he couldn't take in the fact that they'd actually arrived at their destination. Only when a couple of girls appeared on the far side of the clearing, and started whooping too, did Kid grasp that this was it. This was Caracol. The city centre. They were there.

One of the girls was Tilda. She came running across the clearing, crying, 'Joanne . . . Jake . . . Al . . . Wallace . . . Snow . . . Kid . . . Hal . . . You've arrived! *But where's Fritz?*'

Kid stopped laughing at that. People were explaining about Fritz, and suddenly he felt to blame again. Fritz would have loved this place. The other girl was running too, and there were others behind her, drawn by the din. Even Candy was there, and

Doc Rose, and Laydee, Jim and Benji. The boundary cutters had beaten them by an hour but they weren't crowing about it. They had something else on their minds, and it wasn't winning.

It was food.

'We need noodles,' they said as soon as they'd finished greeting each other. 'We've had spiders in ours, making cobwebs and laying eggs. And our powdered milk is low, and so are coffee granules, proper tea and sugar. God, we're missing sugar. And as for baked beans – we've been dreaming of baked beans. We could *kill* for baked beans.'

Hal said they could forget the baked beans and, if they wanted to know why, they should ask Jaguar-Boy here. Kid felt himself flush. Everybody turned to him and he felt to blame yet again. Kid and Candy exchanged looks.

'Never mind the baked beans. At least for now. Come and see where we're staying,' Candy said. 'Come on, all of you. It's our camp for the next two nights. And it's got proper beds.'

The camp was on loan to Wide-World Treks from a team of archaeologists who used it for digs. It had a kitchen with a proper stove, properly dug toilets, tables and chairs and a bunkhouse full of beds.

'There's even a road,' Candy said. 'Not a tarmac

road, or anything like that. But at least a track for getting vehicles in. It almost feels like we're back in civilisation.'

The road was the hardest to believe. But the sight of a camp built out of shacks with doors and shutters was almost as surreal. Kid stood staring at them. Only moments ago, he'd been in deepest jungle, miles from anywhere, now he felt like a tourist arriving at some resort.

But Caracol had attractions that the ordinary resort could only dream of. Maybe they didn't include things like swimming pools and en-suite bathrooms, but they did include an entire kingdom of hidden temples and palaces, gradually unfolding as the group moved round the site.

Kid wandered across a series of grassy plazas surrounded by white stone structures. Jez pointed out the site of an ancient observatory where the Maya would have studied the stars. He showed them sculpted reliefs, and explained what they meant. He took them on a tour of palaces, each one larger than the last. Finally he led them to a grassy ball-court, which he couldn't wait to tell them about.

'What sorts of games would have been played here?' Star Wars Al asked.

'Ones to celebrate great victories in battle,' Jez replied. 'But unlike our games they'd have gone on for days. And also, unlike our games, they'd have been played using the Mayans' conquered enemies' heads.'

Everybody looked disgusted, but Jez had only just started. 'Don't you want to know what the winner's prize would be?' he said.

People weren't sure that they did, but Jez told them anyway. 'The winner would have been sacrificed to the gods,' he said. 'It was the highest honour, apparently, because the gods only wanted the best.'

It was hard to believe that this sunny plaza once had been a place of blood and death. Kid walked away. Caracol was full of ghosts. He shivered. Perhaps he didn't like it so much after all.

Snow came up to him. 'You know who'd have loved all this? Poor old Fritz. It isn't fair,' she said.

'Tell that to the ancient Mayan ball-court winners whose prize was to be sacrificed,' Kid said.

'I'm being serious,' she said.

'Well, don't be,' he said.

As they walked along together, Snow linked her arm through his. It didn't feel awkward, not as if she was coming on to him or anything like that. It was simply what it was – a casual act of friendliness. Together they strolled through the rest of the plazas exploring temples, and Kid knew that things between them had been restored. The bad feelings over what he'd said to Fritz were finally laid to rest between them.

Snow went on about life in Mayan times, wanting to know more. This was a subject she returned to later over supper. What had happened to the inhabitants of Caracol? she wanted to know. Where were their descendants now?

Most of them had died, Jez said, but some still lived in Belize to this day. 'Those of you who'll be taking up placements in Toledo District will be living in their villages,' he said.

A general conversation sprang up about placements, where people were going and what they'd be doing afterwards. Some weren't taking up placements at all, but heading off to Spanish language school in Guatemala. Then others were going backpacking round South America. Then others were heading out to the cayes to learn to dive. And the rest of them were aiming to fly straight home.

Kid wondered what he'd do when his time in Chiquibul was over. It was the first time in ages that he'd thought that far ahead. But whatever happened next, he decided, it could never better this.

The stars shone down upon Caracol and the moon made its temples and palaces glow like silver.

Perhaps it wasn't just a place of blood, Kid thought. Perhaps it was a place of peace as well. A place where people had made their homes, and lived in families, and cared for each other and the world around them, enjoying all the good things in life.

The sense of peace Kid felt, just thinking about things like that, overwhelmed him. It came to him that nothing in his life would ever better this place. But then Hal had to go and spoil it.

'So, Jaguar-Boy, how about you?'

Kid felt himself stiffen. 'How about me *what*?' he said, turning to face Hal.

'When your free ride's finally over, who'll you latch on to next?' Hal said.

Kid felt himself flinch. Hal's choice of words had scored a hole-in-one. He smirked as if he could sense the damage he had done, even if he didn't know its details. Kid's fists tightened, but Jez stepped in.

'There's been no free ride,' he said. 'Hal, what are you on about? Kid's worked his passage. He's worked harder than anyone.'

Everyone agreed, but nothing could be the way it was before. Hal mouthed the words *Jaguar-Boy* again and everybody looked embarrassed.

'What's his problem?' they said, after Jez had dragged him off. 'Don't listen to him, Kid. Pay him no attention.'

But Hal's words had been an insult, and Kid couldn't forget them. They hung in the air, like a challenge to a fight.

19

THE FIGHT

Kid hated Hal after that. He didn't just hate him for spoiling his special moment. He hated him for everything – his piggy eyes, his sweaty face, his naggy, whining voice. Everything about him kept Kid awake, lying in his first proper bed for weeks, but totally unable to sleep.

Something had been building up for weeks and now, here in this place of blood not peace, where even winners ended up being sacrificed to the gods, it had finally come spilling out.

Early next morning, Kid slipped out of bed, leaving all the other fresh-faced sleepers with their mumbles and snores. With nothing better to do, he decided to climb Caracol's highest building, the pyramid-shaped temple known as El Caana. It was obviously going to be a tricky undertaking, but Kid didn't care.

He started climbing, geckos scuttling ahead of him and scorpions hurrying out of his way. To begin with, his ascent was no more difficult than climbing a flight of stairs without a hand-rail. But slowly the steps became taller and the ground became smaller and further away, and Kid started feeling as if he was tackling a mountain.

Half way up El Caana, much to his relief, he found a grassy plaza where he could stop. By now morning was breaking across the sky, but the forest still lay in darkness, and so did Caracol, the tops of its temples protruding through the forest canopy like a dark fleet floating on an even darker sea.

Kid could see the canopy flowing away from him, all the way to the horizon. Slowly colour was creeping into it in little eddies, creating swirling shapes which seemed to breathe with life. Kid swore he could see faces out there in the growing light – pale faces, like the ghosts of all the people who had lived here once and, like him, lost out in the game of life.

Kid started climbing again. If anyone had asked what he was doing, he couldn't have said. But when he reached the top and found Hal waiting for him, he knew exactly why he'd come.

Just as Hal did too. 'Come up for the view, did you?' he smirked, as if he'd been waiting for this moment all night long.

No, I came to beat the hell out of you, Kid thought. But he didn't say it. Instead he said, 'What've I ever done to you?'

Hal snorted. 'That's just typical,' he said. 'You, you, you – everything's always about you. But, seeing as you've asked, I had a nice view until you came along. But then I also had friends until you came along. And now they're your friends and have no time for me.'

Kid said Hal was talking rubbish – everybody was his friend. Hal said *but not Snow, at least not anymore* and Kid asked him what he meant by that.

'You don't fancy her, do you?' he said.

Hal flushed. 'I saw you yesterday, moving in on her,' he said.

Kid said he hadn't been moving in on her, but what if he had? Hal said Snow could do better than someone like him, with nothing in the world but some old cardboard box and a pathetic sob story about his mother being dead.

Kid felt himself go cold all over. 'It isn't a sob story,' he said. 'Every word of it is true. But how d'you know it anyway? You listened in, didn't you? When I was telling Jez, you were eavesdropping.'

Hal said so what? Not that he'd believed a word of it, anyway. It might have fooled Jez, and won Kid a place on the team, but it hadn't fooled him. From that moment onwards, Hal said, he'd been watching Kid, waiting to expose his lies.

'What makes you so sure that they're lies?' Kid demanded to know.

'My parents warned me about people like you,' Hal replied. 'Wide boys. Con men. Sharp talkers. City slickers. They said you can't trust them like honest country folk.'

Kid laughed at that and shook his head. '*Honest country folk*,' he said. 'Is that what you are?'

Hal took a step towards him. Kid warned him to back off and, to show him he meant business, gave him a shove. Undeterred, Hal took another step. This time his fists were clenched.

'I said back off!' Kid said.

'I'll do what I want . . .'

'Not to me you won't!'

'Just you try and stop me, *Jaguar-Boy . . .*'

The two boys stood pressed nose to nose, shouting at each other. Somewhere beneath them, tiny figures appeared from the camp, disturbed by the din and wanting to know what was going on. But the boys didn't see them any more than they saw birds rising from the trees, squawking as if they knew that trouble was on the way.

They were too caught up with each other to notice anybody else. Kid shouted that if Hal called him Jaguar-Boy one more time, he'd break his every last bone, and Hal shouted the words back, only louder this time. Then, true to his threat, Kid punched Hal in the chest amid a roaring sound inside his head, which cried out, 'Yes . . . yes . . . *yes!*'

It was a blow for victory. A blow for Kid's pride. A blow for city slickers everywhere, against stupid, bumpkin country boys. Hal reeled back, obviously in pain, but the voice inside Kid still cried *yes* and, when he struck Hal again, causing him to lose his balance, the voice was almost singing.

Hal missed his footing. He started falling down a long flight of steps. Kid should have tried to save him, but he scrambled after him instead, continuing the attack. All the way down the steps he kept it up, aiming blows at Hal and Hal trying to aim a few back whilst fending Kid off. This was the fight they'd both been waiting for. Neither of them was able to stop.

Only when Hal hit the plaza halfway down the pyramid – hit it hard and didn't get up – did the fight finally stop. Hal lay where he'd fallen, and Kid wanted to punch him again and call him a coward for pretending. But blood started coming out of Hal's nose, and his eyes were closed and slowly it began to dawn on Kid how much damage he'd inflicted.

He stepped back in horror. Was Hal dead? Suddenly he found Hubert pulling him away, and Cassie and Doc Rose surrounding Hal. Jez was there too, and Candy, all of them leaning over Hal.

After that, things happened very fast. For the second time in just a few weeks, an air ambulance had to be radioed for, to take Hal to hospital. The last Kid saw of him was a white face smiling through the pain with the satisfaction of knowing what he'd achieved.

Sure enough, when Hal had gone, Jez took Kid aside. He didn't want to know what had started the fight because it made no difference. Wide-World Trekkers International, to give the company its full name, had a zero-tolerance policy on fighting.

'No violence. No way. No chances. No warnings,' said Jez. 'There are other ways of dealing with people you have problems with. You break the rules and you're out.'

'Out?' Kid said.

'*Out*,' Jez said, looking grim.

'You mean . . .?' Kid said.

'I mean I have no choice,' Jez said. 'You can't stay in this team. I'm sorry. I've radioed field-base and Craig's driving out to collect you. It's over, Kid. You'd better get packed and make your farewells.'

20

NICE WEIRD

Beneath the jungle canopy, the track lay hidden like a secret creek. Craig reckoned no one had used it since the last time the archaeologists had been through months ago. The journey back was going to take a long time, he said, and in places it was going to be tricky, so they'd better get going.

People said goodbye, but couldn't quite look Kid in the eye. Snow hugged him hard. She tried to hide her tears, but it was obvious how upset she was. Kid climbed into the Land Rover and Craig set off. Kid looked back once and everyone was waving. He wasn't a one for tears but that last sight of them all made him want to cry.

It was a tricky road, full of ruts and potholes. Craig navigated like a helmsman steering through dangerous waters, his palms on the wheel, spinning it first one way, then the other. Nothing seemed to bother him, no matter how rough the going became or how much the Land Rover tossed and lurched.

Kid shivered at the thought of what news might be waiting from the hospital by the time they arrived back at the field-base. Craig drove in silence as if he'd decided to keep his counsel to himself, at least for now. The Land Rover pitched and rolled, forcing its way between the trees. Kid closed his eyes, trying to block out the sight of the Chiquibul Forest, mile by mile, disappearing behind him.

On a couple of occasions the Land Rover became stuck and Kid had to get out and push. Finally it reached the Macal Bridge, where Kid had first met everybody. Here Craig stopped to let the engine cool and Kid looked downriver, feeling as though the last weeks in the forest had never happened and somewhere down there, drunk on whisky in that ruined shack, was the boy he once had been – his old self back again.

Kid closed his eyes. He felt as if time was trying to rein him in. It tugged at him, playing with his memory, telling him he was still that boy who'd thought he'd find a father in Belize.

When the Land Rover was ready, Craig set off again. The Macal Bridge disappeared and the past was just that, Kid thought – in the past. The river was gone, and so was his father. His naive hopes were gone, and the Chiquibul Forest was history.

The landscape was changing, hour after hour, turning from rainforest to pine tree country, and new hills opening out, waiting to be crossed. Craig continued to drive in silence and Kid's thoughts returned to Hal, knowing that nothing he did or said could ever put things right.

Craig drove them through a couple of villages, which even had electricity pylons and a few cars, despite the road still being an earth track. Then Kid caught a glimpse of the Night Falls Lodge turn, much to his surprise and, the next thing he knew, they were turning on to the Western Highway, heading in the direction of San Ignacio.

Here, driving on a properly paved road again, Craig managed a small smile. Houses appeared, and a couple of cinder-block supermarkets. Kid caught a glimpse of a church tucked down between orange groves, then some more houses – a whole cluster of them this time. Then the Land Rover turned by a petrol station on to another unpaved track lined with houses and trees. At the end of the road stood a tall wooden building painted orange and white, protected by a high, barbed-wire fence.

Craig pulled up outside it, and unlocked a pair of double gates. He drove through, then locked them from inside. Kid felt like a prisoner arriving to serve out his sentence. A woman appeared on a balcony at first-floor level. She was small and thin, with fuzzy brown hair and copper-coloured skin. Craig leapt upstairs to greet her, asking, 'Any messages?' Kid trailed behind, seemingly forgotten until the woman turned back before going inside, and said that supper was ready. In fact, it had been for a while.

'I'm Jasmine, by the way,' she said. 'Welcome to the Wide-World field-base.'

She smiled when she said that. It was the first proper smile Kid had seen all day. But what if she was only smiling because she had bad news to break? Kid's thoughts returned to Hal.

'What's the latest at the hospital?' he asked.

Jasmine beckoned him to follow her indoors. 'Hal's had some X-rays,' she said. 'He's got some nasty bruises but amazingly no cracked ribs. But the hospital's keeping him in because he's got a thumping headache – I mean, a really thumping headache – and they want to keep an eye on it. His parents have been informed of course. Like us, they're waiting to hear more. The nurse I spoke to says he's comfortable, but then that's what they always say.'

Supper was a dismal affair. Craig spent the whole time going through his messages, scarcely noticing what he was eating, Jasmine kept getting up to answer the phone, and not even the surprise appearance of Fritz, hobbling in on sore feet, managed to cheer things up.

'I've been an idiot,' Kid said, when the two of them had finished eating and were sitting out on the balcony.

'In other words, you've done it again,' said Fritz.

'I hate myself,' Kid said.

'Nobody should do that,' Fritz said. 'It's a waste of time and takes up too much energy.'

'But you and I . . .' said Kid.

' . . . are mates who fell out,' Fritz said. 'That's all. We'll get over it.'

They sat in silence after that. Kid thought he didn't deserve a friend like Fritz, who was prepared to put the past behind him with such ease.

'If Hal dies, I'll be sent to prison as a murderer,' he said.

'Don't be so dramatic,' Fritz said. 'Nobody's died yet from a few bruises. Besides, if I had to choose between prison or rotting feet, I know which I'd choose. On the subject of which, do you want to take a look?'

It broke the ice. Fritz started unwrapping his bandages, and Kid told him he could smell his feet and that was enough, thank you very much. Fritz said he'd been an idiot, he could see that now, but it was good to know he wasn't the only one.

'It could be weeks before I get back into the jungle,' he said. 'If at all. I think about the team all the time, feeling like I've let everyone down. Craig and Jasmine give me jobs to do, but I didn't come out to Belize to update some log or man the phones. I feel so useless and pathetic.'

That night the two of them shared a dormitory behind the operations room, which they had all to themselves. As Kid fell asleep, he thought about how fast things could change. Only a night ago he'd been in Caracol, looking forward to weeks more in the jungle. Now what did he have to look forward to?

Next morning he didn't have to wait long to find out. After breakfast, Craig called him into the operations room. Hal was fine, he said. The hospital had phoned saying he was ready to be discharged. But before driving to Belize City to collect him, Craig wanted to hear what Kid had to say for himself.

Kid had known this would be coming at some point, and had tried to prepare himself. It had given him something to do in the long hours of the night. But facing Craig, everything he'd planned rang hollow. 'It wasn't my fault.' 'He started it.' 'He got me all wound up.' Given what he'd done, how petty was that?

Kid sat in silence, unable to look up. 'All right, then,' said Craig. 'If you've nothing you want to say, let me tell you what Wide-World thinks of people who use their fists to settle disputes. Acts of violence aren't what we're about. They totally undermine what we're trying to achieve. It's not just the person who's attacked who gets damaged. The whole group gets damaged, and so does the attacker too. In other words, what you did wasn't just stupid. It wasn't just mindless. It belittled you. Your standing in the group is diminished by what you've done. Everybody thought so well of you – *but not any more.*'

Kid hung his head. He waited to be shown the door. 'I'm sorry,' he mumbled.

Craig said he wasn't the one who needed apologising to and, if Kid really meant it, he could say so to Hal when he returned.

'In the meantime,' he said, 'here's a list of jobs that you could do while I'm away. I'll be gone most of the day. It would be nice if they were finished by the time I come back.'

Kid worked flat out. He saw the list as a challenge which he was determined to meet. Even so he still hadn't got through everything when the Land Rover pulled into the compound. Hal was sitting next to Craig, bruises on his face and a swollen, shiny-looking nose. When he saw Kid looking at him, he turned away. But when he'd eased himself out of his Land Rover seat, he came straight over.

'I hoped you'd still be here,' he said, not quite able to look Kid in the eye.

'Why would you hope that?' Kid said, hoping he didn't sound as nervous as he felt.

Hal took a deep breath. 'Because it takes two to make a fight,' he said.

He stuck out his hand. Kid stared at it. He didn't know what to do. He'd prepared himself to make some sort of humiliating but deserved apology, but he hadn't prepared himself for this. Craig stood next to the Land Rover watching him. Jasmine stood on the balcony and Fritz stood next to her. Kid flushed. Did Hal mean this, or was he putting on a show?

Kid said that he was sorry for his part in the fight, and Hal mumbled back that he was sorry too, then quickly shook his hand and excused himself. For all the air of awkwardness between them, supper was easier that night. Hal was quiet and so was Kid. But Craig was full of news regarding next year's projects, Fritz was full of jokes and Jasmine produced a triple-layer chocolate cake the likes of which Kid hadn't seen since arriving in Belize.

After he'd stuffed himself and could eat no more, he went out on to the balcony to do the final job on his list, which was repairing mosquito nets. Hal followed him, volunteering to help. Hal had sewn before with a needle and thread, but Kid hadn't, and he showed him how to do it. There was none of the old swagger though, none of the desire to show Kid up. It was as if a thunderstorm had blown over and the air had finally cleared.

Fritz came and joined them, and for a while all three of them sewed in silence. Then suddenly Hal said, 'You weren't lying, were you, about your mother being dead and having nothing in the world but a cardboard box?'

Taken aback, Kid admitted that he might have been exaggerating slightly. 'I do actually have a bit of cash, thanks to some relative who paid me to go away,' he said.

'But your mother,' Hal said. 'That bit was true?'

Kid said it was. Hal said he felt ashamed. He'd been doing a lot of thinking while he was in hospital, and he'd been talking to Craig too, and he didn't like what had come out.

'I treated you badly,' he said. 'No excuses. I gave you a hard time.'

Kid was surprised. In Hal's shoes, he'd never have owned up to that.

'I don't know how you can say that. You're the one who got pushed down a pyramid,' he said.

'But I'm the one who asked for it,' Hal said. 'We both know that.'

Again silence fell between them as they sewed. Then, for no particular reason that he could explain, Kid went and dug out his parents' photograph. This was his father, he said, and this was his mother and this – brandishing a squashed bundle of feathers that had seen better days – was her hat.

Hal and Fritz both burst out laughing when they saw the hat, and Fritz put it on. 'Your mother never really wore this!' he said.

'On her wedding day,' said Kid.

The three of them cracked up. Parents were weird, they all agreed. Hal said he missed his more than he could say.

'Every day I miss them,' he said. 'The pain's like a toothache that won't go away.'

Fritz said that Hal was lucky to have parents like that. 'My father died when I was six,' he said, 'and I went to boarding-school so long ago that I've forgotten what it's like to miss anybody. At least, I thought I had until I started missing you lot.'

Hal said he'd never been anywhere, let alone away to school. In fact, that was why his older brothers and sisters had clubbed together to send him here, reckoning it was bad for him to have never met anyone he hadn't grown up with, gone to playgroup and school with, or worked with on the family farm.

'This was meant to be a treat,' Hal said, 'but I found it really hard, especially at first. It wasn't the jungle that bothered me. It was the people. I'd never met a black man before, except on the telly of course, or a boarding-school boy, or a Dutch girl or a Goth. I'd never met anyone like Jez, who'd travelled round the world. And I'd definitely never met anyone like you, Kid, so oozing with self-confidence.'

Kid rolled his eyes. 'So *what*?' he said. 'Self-confidence? You must be joking!'

'I'm not, 'Hal said. 'Nothing ever throws you. Not jaguars, not *xateros*, not even coming to Belize all on your own.'

Kid said things threw him all the time – it was just that he'd had years of practice in hiding it. It was hard owning up to a thing as deeply engrained as that, but then it was hard for Hal too, to admit to envying Kid for seeming so cool.

Finally even Fritz got in on the act, saying that he didn't own a castle, no matter what the gossip-mongers said. And as for becoming a lord, his granddad was the one with the title, not him, and he was pretty fit, so it would be years before it came Fritz's way.

The truth was really coming out. The three of them grinned at each other. Kid wanted to know if Fritz's family really had it in for him like Tilda had said. Fritz said that unfortunately, in his family, everybody had it in for everybody else. Then Hal admitted that he did fancy Snow, and had been lying when he said he didn't. Then, seeing as the other two had been so open, Kid told them both about his mother – how she'd been dead for days on a cocktail of pills and alcohol, and he'd been the one who'd found her and he'd never been able to get the sight out of his mind.

This was something Kid had never told anybody, not even Nadine. But then he'd never sat round like this before, or been in a situation so intimate or trusting. It felt weird, he thought, but it was a nice weird.

The phone rang inside the house. Kid heard Jasmine's voice behind the screen door. Up in the trees cicadas whistled and night birds whooped. The stars were out above the house and Kid could see the moon rising above the San Ignacio rooftops. It was good to be here, he thought.

At least it was until Craig came out on to the balcony, his face stretched into a smile which definitely didn't reach his eyes.

'It's good to hear the three of you on speaking

terms again,' he said, in a sad, slow, weary voice. 'But I'm afraid I'm the bearer of bad news. Fritz, why's it always got to happen to you? There's been a car accident and your family want you home. Your mother's fine, and so's your grandmother, but your grandfather was at the wheel, and I'm sorry to have to tell you that he died on impact.'

PART FIVE

BLUE BANK SPRINGS

21

PARTING GIFT

Fritz flew home next morning. Craig helped him book his flight, then drove him to the airport, leaving Jasmine to transport Hal out to Gold Mine for Hubert to collect him. Hal was delighted to be thought well enough to rejoin the team, but angry and embarrassed that Kid wasn't being allowed back too.

Kid said he was the one who'd struck the first blow so it made perfect sense for him to be the one who wasn't trusted any more. But Hal pointed out that he'd been the real aggressor, winding Kid up with words instead of fists.

'I'm afraid rules are rules,' said Jasmine, getting into the Land Rover. 'It isn't in anybody's power to change them. And, besides, there's the little matter of Kid not being a proper, paid-up, signed-for and insured volunteer.'

It was a miracle, apparently, that Jez had managed to keep Kid on the project for as long as he had. But after what Kid had done, there was no way he could twist the rules any further. Kid watched Jasmine driving Hal away. Despite his brave words, he felt pretty bad. After all, the bunkhouse wasn't just a project. It was a home. And the team weren't just fellow-volunteers. They were family.

When the Land Rover had completely disappeared, pulling on to the highway, Kid let himself out of the compound and started mooching along the road, feeling like a lost dog, kicking cans and raising dust. He'd been asked to stay in and man the phones, but he was too restless to stay still. Children watched him as he walked by. He said hello to them, but they ran away. Then a car came along, and he stepped out of the road to let it by, only for the driver to lean out of the window, calling out, 'It's the lost boy – well, I'll be damned!'

It was Taxi-May. She switched off the engine and leapt out of the car to give Kid an unexpected hug. She'd been worrying herself silly, she said, about the way she'd left him up at Night Falls Lodge.

'I went back asking after you a few days later,' she said. 'They told me you'd moved on, but I could tell it wasn't as straightforward as that. Sure enough, a couple of weeks later, I saw one of those Night Falls girls in Mrs Edie's place, trying to sell a rucksack full of boy's clothes which I just knew were yours.'

Kid marvelled that anyone should remember him, let alone give a damn about his clothes.

'Did anybody buy anything?' he asked.

'Not in Mrs Edie's they didn't because she chased them out,' Taxi-May said.

Kid thought about that girl up at Night Falls Lodge. He imagined taking the police up there and getting her arrested – Dave the American, and Marky too. It would be his revenge. But the police, he guessed, wouldn't be interested. And, besides, revenge was a waste of energy. Kid could see that now. So, his clothes were gone. But there'd always be new clothes, and at least he'd survived to tell the tale.

Taxi-May's car radio cackled, and she was called away. Kid returned to the field-base and spent the rest of the day either in the operations room playing on the computers or in the dormitory, sorting out what was his and what was Wide-World's, so that when they sent him packing he'd be ready to leave.

Kid also spent some time on the internet, trying to plan an itinerary. There were plenty of places in Belize that he hadn't visited yet. Beaches down the south coast that everybody raved about. Cayes out on the reef where people went diving. Towns and villages which were good for music, apparently, not to say anything of fantastic cooking.

Craig returned from the airport, bringing a note which Fritz had written Kid just before he'd left. But Kid didn't want to read it, and refused to even take it. In the last few days, everything had been stripped away from him. First the project had been stripped away, then his first ever proper family, then the forest had been stripped away, then even his rucksack with everything he'd brought out from England, apart from a few personal effects including a stupid hat. Now even his last two friends had been stripped away. And it had all happened at the speed of lightning.

Craig tried again. 'This is important. You should read it,' he said, thrusting the note at Kid.

'I don't want to.'

'*Read it.*'

Craig stuffed the note into Kid's hands and walked away. But still Kid refused to read it until later, on his own. He went and sat in the empty dormitory, and wondered where Fritz was now and how far he'd gone on his flight, and then he unfolded the note and started scanning down the lines, still not reading them properly – until something forced him to stop.

What was this? What was Fritz saying here? Kid

went back to the beginning and started again.

I want to give you something, Fritz had written. You've been a good mate. You always laugh as if my jokes are funny, even when they're not. One day I hope we'll meet again, but it won't be in Belize. And that means there'll be a placement coming up soon, if you're interested, with a Kekchi-Mayan family, living with them and teaching in their school. Everything's been paid for, so you wouldn't have to worry about that. And seeing as I won't be able to take it myself, I've talked to Craig about Wide-World letting you go instead. Apparently it's okay as long as you're insured. And as long as your placement isn't anywhere near Hal. Craig reckons that living with the Kekchi-Mayans might be good for you, and you might be good for them. I'm not sure what he means by that, but what do you think? The placement's yours, if you want. Have it on me. My parting gift.

22

A BUS RIDE

The bus was packed mostly with Belizeans, though there were a few lone tourists with rucksacks piled up at the back. Its windows were wide open and its seats covered with dust off the road. Kid sat by the window, his face pressed against the glass, his mind rolling back over everything that had happened since he'd read Fritz's note.

That Fritz had offered him his placement was something that Kid still couldn't quite believe. And that Wide-World Treks had gone along with it was hard to believe too. But, with a bit of arm-twisting from Craig, they had, and some special pleading from Jez, who'd been on the radio to say it was a crying shame about the fight with Hal because Kid was a good, hard worker whom everybody liked and who'd made it his business to fit in. The way he'd come out to Belize all on his own was an act of courage that deserved acknowledging. And, from a man like Jez, Craig said, you couldn't ask for higher praise.

The bus set off, and Kid wondered what he was in for. He tried to imagine the people waiting for him at the other end. If I can cope with the jungle, he thought, I can cope with this. And if I can survive a jaguar, I can survive anything.

Kid's stomach churned. Craig had assured Kid that the Kekchi-Mayans would speak English, but what sort of English? Would he understand it? And how would he get on with them, staying in their village for two whole months?

Normally Kid wouldn't have minded about meeting new people, but he was anxious not to let Craig down, and all the other people who'd put their faith in him. He closed his eyes and tried to sleep. At Belmopan he awoke as food sellers came down the aisle, selling homemade wares. He fell asleep again and didn't awaken until the bus was on the Hummingbird Highway, heading down to a town called Dangriga which was where most of the tourists left the bus, heading south for the sandy beaches of Placencia.

The people who boarded at Dangriga were black-skinned Garifuna people whose ancestors were Africans, and whose language they'd brought with them. The way they spoke had nothing to do with the Kriol Kid had picked up in the jungle and in Belize City. Listening to them, he felt as if he was being taken ever-deeper into an unknown world. The bus had a new driver now, and reggae was his music.

As soon as it started up, the whole bus erupted. Fists were raised and cheers went up. The woman across the aisle from Kid leant across to explain in English that that he was listening to Lucky Dube, that giant among reggae artists who'd recently been shot dead.

'What, here in Belize?' Kid said, looking shocked.

'In South Africa,' the woman said, pronouncing the 'Africa' with a 'u', not an 'a'. 'But he still our brudder.'

It didn't take long for Kid to decide that Lucky Dube was his brother too. Of all the reggae the driver played on that long journey south, his music was the best. When he sang, the whole world came alive. How could anyone, Kid thought, who sounded as real as sunshine was – anyone whose voice was so alive and powerful and warm and strong – possibly be dead?

Kid rolled south in a state of grace, Serious Reggae Music ringing in his head. Sometimes the road was lined with pink flowering trees. Once he caught a glimpse of great blue crags, which he guessed must be the Maya Mountain, outlined against the sky.

At the Cockscombe Basin Jaguar Reserve, the bus picked up a white-haired European woman with a rucksack, and her companion, a younger man with an Indiana Jones-style hat. Further on, it stopped for a couple of Mestizo men decked out in gold chains, looking more like pirates than hitchhikers. Then the bus became stuck behind a citrus truck that had broken down, and everybody had to get out to help push it out of the way, rewarded for their efforts with handfuls of grapefruit.

By now the mountains had disappeared from sight and the bus had entered a region of lush citrus groves. Through the open window, Kid smelled something smoky which had about it an unexpected fruitiness which reminded him more of blackcurrants than citrus fruit. For miles he watched orange and grapefruit groves flying past, and then the jungle took over again.

They were heading directly south now, along a paved track called the Southern Highway. A wild exuberance seemed to grip the landscape, which was lush, green and uninhabited for mile after mile. When the first thatched, Kekchi-Mayan house appeared, it came as a surprise.

The bus slowed down for speed bumps, which meant that a village was approaching, and Kid caught sight of a shack with the words KILL YU SPEED painted on it in big white letters. Beyond the shack, he saw a man on a bike leading a horse, and then a woman walking down the middle of the road as if no traffic ever came along. Even when the bus honked at her, she wouldn't move.

The bus veered round her, honking wildly, then round a crowd of boys playing football on the road, then suddenly there was the village, tucked away between the trees. Kid saw wooden, thatched houses built straight on to the earth, chickens and dogs running about, women watching from doorways and children swinging from trees. There were no cars anywhere, and no cables running between houses hinting at electricity.

Kid watched the people in their doorways as the bus went by – men in dusty working clothes and women in brightly coloured dresses trimmed with lace. Nobody acknowledged his gaze or smiled back when he smiled at them. He could have been an apparition from another world as far as anybody was concerned.

Beyond the village, the made-up road gave out, turning from concrete paving to beaten earth. Immediately, everybody started to be thrown about and dust came in through the windows in red clouds. A series of other villages went by, all thatched like the first. If Kid had wondered if life down south was really going to be different, here was his answer. Each time a village approached, he wondered if it was his home for the next two months, Blue Bank Springs. Once or twice he even made to get off, but the driver stopped him, saying he'd tell him when he arrived.

For the first time since Belmopan, Kid's stomach started knotting and he asked himself what lay ahead. The bus passed a village called Five Falls and another called Golden Stream. Kid pressed his face against the window, wanting to get a closer look at them. But the white-haired European woman across the aisle chose this moment to announce that she was a writer, travelling with her son, and to start telling him her life's history.

Kid imagined ending up like her – travelling on a bus somewhere, looking for stories, unable to stop. Half of him was horrified at the idea of not having a home, but half of him warmed to not staying long enough to ever mess up.

A few miles down the road, another village appeared. This time it really was Blue Bank Springs. The driver pulled up. Kid grabbed his brand-new rucksack, which was a parting gift from Craig and

Jasmine, and started up the aisle.

'Good luck,' called the writer, as if she thought Kid might need it.

Kid didn't answer. A man had boarded the bus and was watching him approach. He was short and slim, with high cheekbones, dark almond-shaped eyes and a thick mop of black hair.

'Are you Kid?' he said in English.

Kid nodded. 'Yes,' he said.

The man helped Kid down off the bus, taking his rucksack. Kid was aware of everybody watching them. He stood on the side of the road, not knowing what to say, overwhelmed with shyness for the first time in his life. The man beamed at him. There was nothing hidden in his face.

'Welcome to our village,' the man said. 'I'm Reuben. I am your host. I'm happy to meet you. I hope you will be happy living here in Blue Bank Springs with us.'

23

REUBEN'S FAMILY

This was it. Kid's village. Kid's host. His next two months. There could be no going back. No going anywhere because the bus had disappeared in a cloud of dust.

Kid shouldered his rucksack and followed Reuben up a grassy track. The house they were heading for had one window with a single wooden shutter tied back with string, two doors which faced each other and were open, a bench along its front wall, a bird-house and a flag-pole sporting the colours of the new government party, the UDP.

As they approached, children from all over the village came running to greet them. Kid was danced around as he stepped over the threshold into a huge, cool space created by a vaulted thatch high above his head. Whole trees had been cut down to provide the labyrinth of timbers for supporting that thatch.

'Welcome to my home,' Reuben said.

A shy-looking woman stepped forward. She was Reuben's sister and her name was Renata. The small boy clinging to her legs was Reuben's son. Kid smiled at him and he smiled back, his face full of mischief. His name was Renaldo and he was four years old. His sister's name was Juanita, and she was just a baby. Their mother's name was Lydia. She emerged from a screened-off corner of the room that contained a bed. She was wearing a cotton dress patterned with brightly coloured flowers. Kid thought she looked like a queen, her thick hair twisted into a knot on the back of her head and her baby in her arms, shiny and contented. She greeted Kid shyly, but there was something proud about her all the same.

'This is my wife,' said Reuben.

Kid said, 'I'm pleased to meet you,' and smiled nervously.

'You're welcome. I hope you will be happy in our home,' said Lydia.

Kid looked around. Blue Bank Springs was every bit as different as he'd imagined, but home was home wherever you went. He looked at the old string hammocks strung from beam to beam, the collection of small tables covered with oil-cloths, the pans hung from nails in the wall and the shelves stacked full of spices. All of them gave off a sense of homeliness. It might take a while, he thought, but he'd be all right here.

A fire was lit for supper in the open hearth, smoke rising through the thatch. Renata said she had some baking to do, and Lydia retired with baby Juanita back behind the screen, leaving Reuben to show Kid where to put his rucksack and where he would be sleeping.

The house was full of children by now, who'd crowded in from all over the village. Reuben said there was time before supper for them to take Kid down to the river to bathe. Immediately – without waiting to see if he wanted to or not – all the children, including Renaldo, swept Kid away. They were plainly curious about this stranger in their midst, who was taller than anybody else and spoke in a tongue that wasn't Kekchi-Mayan. Kid felt as if he'd been caught up in a cloud of bright butterflies, their only means of communication the phrase, repeated over and over again, *was-yur-name?*

A path crossed the village between a string of other houses just like Reuben's – single-storey, thatched dwellings surrounded by palm trees and flowering shrubs. It passed a couple of tin buildings which turned out to be churches, a cluster of brightly painted sheds and an old car without wheels. Beyond the last of the houses was the jungle, and a river flowed out of it, along the back of the village, looping back in again on the other side of the track where the bus had disappeared.

Kid was led down to a shady beach where the children stripped out of their clothes and plunged into the water, calling him to do the same, which he did – plunging in unexpectedly over his head. He came up spluttering to find everybody laughing. The children had known what would happen, of course. They'd led him straight into a deep spring of bubbling water, without a word of warning that it was there.

Kid tried to swim to shallower waters, but the children pulled him back and piled on top of him. Suddenly the quiet river was quiet no longer but alive with shrieks and yells. Children leapt off logs, splashed each other, dive-bombed Kid, and called out incessantly, 'Was-yur-name?' It seemed to be the one English phrase that everybody was confident about. And whatever Kid answered, the question kept coming back

Kid was everybody's friend. He didn't even have to try. More children kept turning up all the time, and other visitors came too – village women with pots that needed washing, and the simply curious who stared without any excuse. They stood between the trees at the top of the bank, keeping their distance as if not wanting to be rude. When Kid looked up to them, they'd wave shyly, and he'd wave back.

But there was nothing shy about the children. Kid returned through the village, dragged along by them as if he was their prize. Everybody wanted him to come to their house, meet their family, see their hens and dogs, share salt plums with them, ride their turkeys and see the trees they swung in when they played. But it was getting dark now. Mothers called their children home, and that included Lydia, standing at the doorway, looking out for Kid and Renaldo.

After Kid had entered the house, Lydia latched the door behind him and shut the wooden shutters to keep the mosquitoes at bay. Toledo District, where Blue Bank Springs was situated, was bad for mosquitoes, she said. Kid would have to watch out, especially at night, if he didn't want to be eaten alive. She lit a couple of candles to drive away the darkness, and Renata served up supper with a torch tucked under her arm so that she'd have free hands.

It was a special meal for Kid's first night. Reuben sat by his side telling him what he was eating. First Lydia brought him a bowl of peppery-flavoured eggs, tomatoes and a cabbage-like substance cut from the heart of the cohune palm, accompanied by freshly-baked corn tortillas stacked beneath a small white cloth. This was washed down with a pinkish, sweet, fruit-flavoured drink that turned out to be chocolate, surprisingly enough. Then a cup full of yellow sticky gruel – more food than drink – was produced, tasting unmistakably of sweetcorn.

'This is *lub*,' Reuben said. 'It's a Kekchi-Mayan drink, and everything you've eaten is Kekchi-Mayan food.'

There was so much to eat that Kid struggled with his meal, not wanting to offend his hosts. Reuben talked all the way through, telling him about Kekchi-Mayan life and his concerns for their people's future. He was an endless fund of knowledge on everything from the wisdom of not paving the tracks that ran through the villages, to the effects of television if electricity should ever come their way.

Finally Lydia – who'd installed herself in one of the hammocks where she was rocking Juanita – called out something in Kekchi-Mayan that brought Reuben's lessons to an abrupt close.

'Lydia thinks I talk too much,' he said. 'She says I shouldn't fill your head with things you won't remember. She says you've had a long day and I'm tiring you. She also says that, if I want you to be happy, I must let you go to bed.'

Lydia smiled from her hammock, as if to say *yes, that's what I said.*

Kid admitted that he was tired, and Reuben showed him outside to the wash-house – a small plank shack, the size of a shower-cubicle – and the long-drop. Kid sat on its rough-hewn seat, the door pulled behind him, listening to geckos scampering about above his head, trying not to think about what else might be up there, hidden in the darkness.

Emerging into the fresh air came as a relief. Kid moved on to the wash-house where he found bowls, jugs, soap and that most Western of all commodities – toothpaste. When he came out, he looked up at the stars. The sky was alive with them and the air around Kid was alive with moving dots of phosphorescent light that were almost emerald green.

Kid had never seen fireflies before. He span round, and everything on every side of him – on earth and in the heavens too – seemed to be starry.

Back in the house, Lydia had retired to bed, taking one of the candles with her, and so had Renata who'd taken Renaldo with her and was curled up with him on a mat beside the open hearth. Only Reuben sat up, wanting to make sure Kid had everything he needed and to wish him a good night.

'I hope you will be happy with us,' he said.

That word again, happy. Kid had never heard it used so many times in just one day.

24

TORTILLAS

Kid awoke before first light to a rumbling noise that seemed to fill the house and make its walls shake. First there was a quick blast of sound, then it stopped, then it started again. Kid checked his watch. It was only five o'clock. Wide awake and curious, he climbed out of his hammock and tiptoed across the floor, anxious not to wake anybody up. At the door, he slipped the latch and crept outside. The sound came from across the village, but he couldn't see where from.

It took Renata, coming up behind him, to explain what was going on. Kid asked what the noise was and she said it came from the electricity generator that powered the corn mill.

'What, at this hour?' Kid said.

Renata smiled. 'This hour is when we grind our corn,' she said, holding up a metal drum. 'That's what I'm doing now. If you want, you can come and see.'

Kid returned inside for his shoes, then followed Renata through the village. The air was mild and soft. It mightn't be light yet, but it was a good time to be out and about. In the distance, he could see the edge of the Maya Mountains standing against the sky, wreathed in veils of mist. Somewhere across the village, a solitary bird set up a sharp *chachalaca* sound.

Kid passed dark houses were people still slept, passed wash-houses, bird-houses and tall silent trees. As he grew accustomed to the darkness, he noticed other shadowy figures up too. Some of them were heading in the same direction as him and Renata, but others were heading down to the track where a truck was waiting for them.

Kid saw figures throwing themselves into the back of the truck and then, headlights blazing, being driven away. Renata explained that they were going to the logging company, which was where most of the village men worked. It was where Reuben worked, she said, but he also worked on his farm and sometimes on his parents-in-law's farm, when they were too sick to do it for themselves.

They'd reached the corn mill by now, and Renata stopped outside to put down her drum. From the sort of noise that had awoken him, Kid had been expecting a substantial building, but the corn mill was just a simple thatched dwelling, no different to all the others in the village. Renata led the way into the darkness inside. As Kid's eyes grew accustomed to the gloom he saw a rickety-looking iron monster, complete with belts and wheels, chains, chutes and a huge bucket-mouth. He also saw the miller – an old woman in a tartan frock, who smiled toothlessly.

Renata introduced Kid to the miller in Kekchi-Mayan. The old woman eyed him with the degree of wariness that he was eyeing her machinery. Kid smiled, and she inclined her head.

'I'm not that scary, am I?' Kid said.

Renata shook her head. The miller wasn't scared of anybody, she said. She handed Kid the drum of corn. The miller gestured for him to step forward.

'What am I meant to do?' Kid said.

Renata gestured for him to tip the corn down the chute into the waiting bucket-mouth, which was hungry to get chomping. He watched as it disappeared in a stream of cream-coloured pebbles, far removed from the soggy yellow sweetcorn that came in cans. The machinery jiggered about and the corn jumped and juddered its way through the system. The air was full of dust. The miller's face was white. Kid had to wipe his eyes, but the pricking that bothered them didn't seem to bother hers.

By now several other women had appeared, standing in the door eyeing Kid shyly. When the mill stopped grinding, Renata introduced him.

'This is our boy,' she said in English, so that Kid would understand. 'His name is Kid. He's going to teach in our school.'

She pronounced it *Keed*. The women tried it out, as if testing it for size. They smiled, said, 'Hello, Keed' carefully, as if they didn't often speak in English, then returned to Kekchi-Mayan. Kid guessed they were talking about him, and wondered what they were saying. Later, leading him back through the village, Renata explained that they'd been commenting on the fact that he looked more Creole than English, teasing her and asking if she was sure she'd been sent the right boy.

Kid smiled at that. He said his father was a Belizean, and explained about coming all the way from England to find him. Renata seemed to find this confusing. Here in Blue Bank Springs, if you didn't have a father, then you lived with your brothers and sisters, or aunties and uncles or at least your *xa-an*, which was the Kekchi-Mayan word for grandmother. That was what had happened to her. When her father had died, and her mother not long afterwards, she'd moved into her brother Reuben's house.

'Don't you ever feel in the way?' Kid asked, thinking about Nadine back in England.

Again Renata seemed to find this confusing. 'Why would I feel that?' she said. 'My brother's home is mine. The only way I'd leave is if I found a husband of my own. Then he'd go into the forest, like Reuben did for Lydia, and cut down trees and build me a house.'

Kid asked if Renata had anybody lined up for this labour of love.

She laughed and shook her head. She was still waiting, she said, but so far no one matched up to Reuben.

'He's a good man,' she said. 'Better to live with a good brother than a bad husband.'

By now, light had broken in the sky, and the village was coming to life. Cockerels hollered. Doors and shutters banged open. Voices called out to each other. Children rushed about, revelling in the cool air before the heat later on. Renaldo came rushing across the grass to greet them, shouting *was-yur-name* over and over like a CD on repeat. Lydia yelled at him to come here and get dressed for school, but he took no notice. She was up and dressed ready to make tortillas for breakfast.

Feeling like a spare part, Kit watched her light the fire, slide an iron griddle over it, then take the freshly milled corn and start turning it to dough. When it came away cleanly from the sides of the bowl, she formed it into little nut-sized pieces which she beat beneath her palms into perfect spheres. Finally, when the griddle was hot enough, she tossed the spheres on to it to cook on both sides, and ended up with tortillas.

Kid watched in silence, impressed by her skill. He'd seen plenty of griddle-action in his time at Jet's, but never anything quite as fast as this. Lydia's hands moved like lightning. By the time the sun had risen high enough to shine into the house, he was seated at the table with his breakfast in front of him. Through the open door, he could see the bird-house where chicks were bathing in an old tyre and an aged turkey was wobbling about. He could also see a bus chundering along the track in a cloud of dust.

It was only the second vehicle Kid had seen that morning, so he watched with interest as it drew to a halt immediately beneath the house. An enormous Creole woman with a bag of books disembarked. She headed up the grassy path towards the houses, and children everywhere disappeared indoors. Her shadow only had to fall across them, and they were gone.

Kid finished eating breakfast and guessed that he should get dressed too. Somewhere in his rucksack was a letter of introduction to Miss Elizabeth Brandon-Atkins, Head Teacher of Blue Bank Springs School. Unless he was mistaken, this person passing through the village, inflicting good behaviour on all its children without a word being said, had to be her.

'That woman,' he said, just to make certain. 'The one who just got off the bus – who is she?'

Renaldo ran round and round, resplendent in grey shorts and a snow-white shirt. Lydia looked up from trying to grab him for long enough to tuck it in. Her expression said it all. *You'll know soon enough,* it said.

But she answered anyway. 'That's Teacher Betty,' she said.

25

TEACHER BETTY

Kid hurried through the village, accompanied by Renaldo. According to him if Teacher Betty rang the assembly bell and he wasn't there, he might as well not bother because he'd be in so much trouble. Kid clutched his letter, his stomach churning for the first time since arriving in Blue Bank Springs. Was Teacher Betty really that fearsome? He hoped not.

The school was a single-storey, tin-roofed, concrete structure built on a ridge above the river. A shady veranda ran along the front of it, facing a flagpole, and it was here that all the pupils were lined up for assembly. They were immaculately dressed, the girls in colourful frocks with not a crease in sight, the boys like Renaldo in shorts and fresh white shirts.

Kid felt scruffy by comparison, and he was late as well. Renaldo ran to join his classmates, but Kid stood to one side as one of the children rang the bell which signalled the raising of the Belizean flag. At this, everybody snapped to attention, hands over their hearts, and started singing their national anthem.

Kid had never been much of a one for patriotism. He thought that things like anthems were a waste of space. To his surprise, however, this anthem contained no gracious queens or glorious victories. This anthem had guts. There were coral islands in it, and blue lagoons, angels, stars and the moon. There were even a few pitched battles thrown in for good measure, and there were invaders being driven back by valiant behaviour.

'O, *Land of the free by the Carib Sea,*' the children began, and, '*For freedom comes tomorrow's noon,*' they finished off.

Kid felt like singing along. Who wouldn't want to, with a swash-buckling anthem like that?

Assembly finished at last, the children filed into their classrooms and the woman whose appearance had caused such a dramatic effect earlier came and introduced herself. As Kid had suspected, she was Miss Elizabeth Brandon-Atkins.

'Named after de Queen,' she explained, adding – in case there was doubt about who she meant – 'Queen Elizabeth II. Once she was yur queen, but now she's ours. Jus' like Bileez. Once it was yurs, but not any more. By de way, you don' have to call me Miz Brandon-Atkins. My staff know me as Teacher Betty, or jus' plain Lizabeth to friends.'

Kid couldn't imagine being a friend of Teacher Betty's. Gripping his shoulder with her enormous hand, she marched him indoors. He tried handing over his letter, but she said she didn't need it. Everything she needed to know about him she'd find out for herself. And she didn't have the time to read letters anyway, because she had important matters to attend to.

' . . . which is why I want yu to meet my class. Yu'll be in charge of dem dis morning.'

Thirty Kekchi-Mayan boys and girls, aged between nine and eleven, stared up at Kid in perfect innocence. He stared back, panic-stricken. Teacher Betty introduced him as Teacher Kid and everybody giggled as if there was something funny about it.

After that, things went downhill quickly. Teacher Betty left Kid with a series of tasks for her class that she obviously didn't think needed explaining. Her parting words of advice to Kid were, 'Dere's nothing to it. Jus' stand dere an' keep order. Dese are Kekchi-Mayan children, which means dere bright. If dere are any problems Teacher Pat next door will help.'

Kid felt sick with apprehension, but there was nothing he could do. Teacher Betty disappeared to attend to whatever was more important than helping acclimatise her latest classroom assistant to teaching, and immediately thirty Kekchi-Mayan children erupted. 'Was-yur-name, was-yur-name, was-yur-name?' they wanted to know, taking it in turns to run up and touch Kid as if he'd just landed from another planet.

He tried to quieten them down, but with no success. Everybody wanted Kid to know how good they were at football, or whose sister, brother, cousin or friend they were, or which house they lived in. They also wanted to nick each other's books and generally lark about. It wasn't long before Kid had to call in the services of Teacher Pat. Not that she was much better at controlling children. Her younger children didn't stay at their desks any more than Kid's older ones did.

In the end, Teacher Betty came storming back, shouting at both classes, 'Yu wan' I beat yu for being naughty?' waggling a ruler at them as if to illustrate what she meant. The din subsided immediately. Obviously Teacher Betty carried out her threats. Books came out and were opened up, and pencils started scratching across pages.

But as soon as Teacher Betty had gone again, the

noise level started rising. Who wanted to do sums when the sun was shining outside, the air was full of clouds of butterflies, half the village dogs were wandering in and out and a new young teacher was in charge?

Nothing Kid did or said could keep his pupils at their desks. By lunchtime he was exhausted and, by the end of the school day, he was sure he'd never make a teacher. Teacher Betty assured him that there was nothing to it once he'd got into his stride. All he had to do was *shout*.

Next day, however, things were just as bad. Even with Teacher Betty in the classroom, the children only had to look at Kid to start mucking about. And the following day, when Teacher Betty put him in with the oldest children in order to help them with their English, things were even worse. For all her insisting that, by their age, they'd all grown up, Kid spent the day with them running amok.

It wasn't just the novelty of a new teacher, he realised. It was him to blame, Teacher Kid himself. He was useless. His pupils didn't muck about because he was a stranger. They mucked about because he was weak.

Kid tried shouting, like Teacher Betty had told him. But, as if they didn't believe he meant it, the children took no notice. He tried getting alongside them and being their friend, but that only made them worse. He even tried toughening up and becoming the teacher from hell. But everybody laughed in his face.

Nothing Kid did made any difference. His mere presence seemed to set the children off. Teacher Betty supervised Kid to see where he was going wrong, and tried correcting his mistakes. But finally she concluded that perhaps he wasn't cut out to be a teacher and his placement in the school had been a terrible misjudgement on somebody's behalf.

Kid felt a fool. Teacher Betty stuck it out for a whole week, but at the beginning of the second week, she put him in a back room out of view of any children and charged him with the task of cataloguing books and making a school library.

Kid set to immediately. Here at last was something useful that he could do. In the morning he organised all the books in sections, listed alphabetically. Then in the afternoon, drawing on his bunkhouse building skills, he put up shelves and arranged the books on them.

By the end of just one day, the library was complete. Teacher Betty had thought she'd got rid of Kid for at least a week. But now here he was, on her hands again – and she plainly didn't know what to do with him.

That afternoon, instead of feeling proud of a job well done, Kid trailed back through the village feeling utterly pathetic. Everybody in Blue Bank Springs had a job to do – the men at the sawmill, the women sitting sewing in their doorways, or nursing their babies. Everybody had a purpose except him. Back in his jungle days, he'd had a purpose, too. But now he felt like a spare part.

Returning home, Kid found Lydia preparing supper and Renata sitting in the shade sewing a shirt which she said was for him. It was a lovely shirt, he said, but he couldn't take it because he hadn't earned it.

'What do you mean?' Renata said.

'Everybody here works,' Kid tried to explain. 'Everybody is useful except for me. I'm beginning to think I ought to leave.'

Renata looked up from the sewing machine. Sometimes her English wasn't very good, she apologised, but she still didn't understand what he meant. Kid explained about school, and how useless he was. In fact, he didn't just feel useless, he said. He felt ashamed.

Lydia came out when Kid said that. So what if he wasn't cut out to be a teacher? That was nothing to be ashamed of, she said.

'But I want to play my part,' Kid said. 'I want you

to be proud of me, and I want to be proud of myself. But here I am, taking your food and hospitality and giving nothing back.'

'But you're our guest.'

'Even so, it isn't fair.'

'Why not?'

'Because you can't afford it. *Because you're poor.*'

Lydia smiled when Kid said that, but went back inside and didn't say another thing. Renata started sewing again and didn't say anything either. Embarrassed to realise that he'd caused offence, Kid would have taken back his words if only he could. But they hung between them all for the rest of the day.

That night, after the candles had been lit and supper eaten, Lydia's father made an appearance. The door opened and in he came, a small, thin man dressed in a patterned shirt of faded cotton. Streaks of grey were mixed up in his black hair, and his face was lined. His name was Joseph, and he was the founder of the village.

'I thought that it was time you and I met,' he said.

Kid sat up straight as if in the presence of royalty. For all that Joseph might look stooped and tired, there was fire in his eyes. Kid only had to look at him to understand his daughter's queenly demeanour. Dimly he was aware of the others sitting up straight too, and even sleepy Renaldo coming back to life.

Joseph pulled up a wooden chair and settled himself in it, right in front of Kid, his hands on his knees. 'I've come to tell you the story of our village,' he said in a quiet, steady voice. 'The story of Blue Bank Springs. It happened like this.

'Before I do a thing I always think. And many years ago I thought to myself, our people grow okra, corn and pumpkins, and we keep pigs and hens but we have nowhere for our own. That was when I came here first to this place. In those days, I worked at the sawmill down at Golden Creek. On the way home, which would take many days, I would sometimes sleep here by the river, and I saw that it was good. I found the spring, which remains clean in the rainy season, even when the rest of the river turns to mud. I tested it, and it was good to drink. And this was a good place to rest. Many times I stopped here on my way back home.

'Then I thought to myself, why not bring our people here? It would be nearer to work for the men, and it has the river of course, and the land is good for farming, and the forest is nearby so we could go and hunt.

'So I went to the government, and I put it to them that they should allow us to settle on this land. And it seemed good to the government too. They allowed me a thousand acres for a village, houses and farms for all our people. So families started coming. Our family came, and other families too, including Reuben's one. They made houses, and took land to farm. Some of them took land by the river, down on the other side of the track. But then the river flooded in the rains and nearly washed them all away. Their cats and dogs, their hens – they all went floating down the river. The water came up to the tops of their houses and we had to take our dories and go and rescue them.

'So no one lives down there any more. We all live up here on the high ground. And I helped to build the Baptist church. I founded it. And other churches were built too, to suit other people's ways of worship. The school was built as well, and more people moved in and we set up a village council to take care of our people and organise the maintenance of our land. We appointed an Alcalde to be our village magistrate and judge all our disputes. The people vote for him. They choose the best man. And, at the minute, that best man is me.

'So that's how we do it here in our village. That's how we live. No one is poor here because we have everything we need. In Belize City we would be poor, and maybe where you come from too, because we'd have no money and everybody there needs money to get on. But here, if we need fish we go and catch it. If we want fruit to eat, we pick it. If we want to go somewhere, we borrow a friend's horse or wait for a truck to come along and put out a thumb.

'We are Mayan people, you know. And once we were the first people in Belize. Before all the others came, we Mayans were already here. And now we're here again, the Kekchi in Toledo District, the Maya-Mopan up round Cayo. Proud Mayan people. All of us.'

26

THE HURRICANE SHELTER

At the end of the following day's school, Kid found a message waiting for him from the village council. Teacher Betty passed it on, trying to hide her relief. It didn't take Kid long to understand why. The village council had requested that Kid be released from his teaching duties in favour of a special project that would benefit the whole of Blue Bank Springs.

The village desperately needed a hurricane shelter. Five years before, a hurricane had flattened half their houses and trees, and it would happen again some day. No one doubted that. They were able and willing to do their own building work but they didn't have money to buy materials. To this end, they wanted Kid to visit the government offices in Belmopan and secure a grant on their behalf. That he'd succeed they seemed to have no doubt. The old government had only ever given money to its friends, but this was *their* government, the one they'd just voted in, and it would hear their application with favour.

Kid tried to take this in. He'd wanted to be useful, and this was his chance – but how to start? Going to Belmopan was all very well, but what to do when he got there? Which government department was he meant to approach? Who was he meant to speak to? And how was he meant to persuade them that he had the authority to act on the village's behalf?

'Who's going to take any notice of me?' he said to Teacher Betty, when he'd read the message through. 'I'm just a kid, and a foreign one too.'

Teacher Betty advised Kid to talk to Reuben, and Reuben advised him to talk to Joseph because he'd secured an entire village for his people and knew more about the government than anybody else. But it was a new government now, Joseph said, and, besides, he couldn't remember which departments he'd visited all those years ago. He was old now, he said. Old and forgetful. But he was sure that if Kid only went to Belmopan the thing would become immediately obvious, especially to an educated person like him.

The following day, Kid gave it his best shot. He didn't have Joseph's confidence, but what else could he do having failed so spectacularly on the teaching front? He started off badly, missing the morning bus, which meant he had to hitchhike instead. Renata sat with him, waiting for a car or truck to come along. It was a long wait too and, by the end of it, she was left in no doubt about how apprehensive he was.

'If I was in your country and I needed help,' she said, 'I'd phone the Queen. She seems like a nice lady. And, because she's queen, she must know everything. So, here in our country, if you don't know what to do, you should do the same.'

'What, phone the Queen?' said Kid.

'No, phone our new Prime Minister, Mr Dean Barrow,' Renata said.

Kid opened his mouth to explain that people like the Queen and the Prime Minister were out of reach to ordinary people, at least they were in England where he came from. But before he could say anything, an open-backed truck pulled up, driven by a dusty American woman with plaited hair who wanted to know where he was heading.

'Belmopan,' Kid said.

'I can give you a ride most of the way there,' she said. 'Jump in the back.'

Kid climbed over the tail-board and settled on a plank bench. Renata stood in the road, waving him off. 'Don't forget,' she said. 'Mr Dean Barrow.'

The day was overcast and no sooner had she disappeared than it turned to rain. Kid thought the American woman might let him into the front seat next to her, but she drove as if she'd forgotten he was there. For miles he bowed beneath the rain, feeling as if he was being flayed by whips. English rain was soft, but Belizean rain felt like iron rods.

Occasionally the woman stopped to pick up other hitchhikers who crammed in together next to Kid, grumbling that the rainy season was coming early this year. Some blamed global warming. Some blamed God. But all of them hoped fervently that the rain would stop before the Southern Highway became waterlogged.

Finally the truck pulled into Dangriga, where the woman dropped Kid off, saying he'd be able to get a bus from here to Belmopan. But the next bus wasn't for a couple of hours, and Kid was left dripping on the sidewalk, looking for somewhere to dry out.

He started walking down the street, darting in and out of doorways, and sheltering under awnings. The road was full of puddles. Those shops which had their wares on the street were covered in tarpaulins.

At the end of the street, Kid found a bar with music playing, no one in it except a man with dreadlocks and a pretty tot of a child. She had the man wrapped round her little finger, fetching drinks and toys for her as if she was a princess. He had to be her father, without a doubt.

Kid went up to the bar and asked for a drink. In London, if he'd walked in dripping wet like that, trailing puddles behind him, he'd have been shown the door. But the man took a Belikin out of the fridge, removed its cap and wrapped it in a napkin. He pushed it across the bar, and Kid paid out of his wallet, which was stuffed with money.

'Keep the change,' he said, like a big man. Why he did that he didn't know.

Three hours later, Kid was still there in that bar, listening to punta rock, telling himself he'd be back there on the street once the rain had stopped. What had happened in all that time, he wasn't at all sure, but his clothes had dried out, the table was full of empty bottles and the bus, he realised glancing at his watch, had long-since gone.

Kid hauled himself to his feet. A shutter had been pulled down in front of the bar and the tables were all empty except for his. The man had disappeared, and so had the little child. It was hours since the morning when Kid had started out, and nothing he'd done since had brought a hurricane shelter for Blue Bank Springs any closer.

Outside on the street, Kid discovered that the rain

had stopped some time ago, and even the puddles had dried out in the baking sun. He started walking along, his legs as heavy as lead, his head spinning as if he'd been drugged. A man approached him, asking for a dollar. It was the first time since Belize City that anyone had done that. Kid automatically went to check his wallet, only to find that it had gone. His pocket was empty. What had happened? Kid didn't know – except that he'd been robbed.

Kid walked straight past the man and carried on along the road, feeling as if everybody was watching him. A woman selling coconut-shell jewellery from a roadside stall asked if he was all right, but he ignored her too and staggered on. He couldn't think straight. He didn't know what to do. What were the chances of his getting his money back if he reported the theft to the police? And what were the chances of his getting out of Dangriga in one piece? He, the canny London boy who thought he knew it all. How had he let this happen to him? Worse still, how was he going to catch a bus to Belmopan with no money to pay his fare?

Feeling a fool, Kid went through his pockets again, as if sure his wallet had to be there somewhere. But all he came up with was a phone card he'd bought when he'd first arrived in Belize City, but had never used. He stuffed it back in his pocket, cursing himself for getting into such a mess. By this time, he was back at the bus terminal, which was thronging with people who all had somewhere to go and the money to pay for it. He turned towards the ticket booth, reckoning his only choice was to try and plead his case, when suddenly – completely out of the blue – the sound of singing came wafting his way.

Kid stopped in his tracks. The singing was as sweet as honey, and yet there was something gravelly about it too. It sounded so alive and personal that Kid expected to find the singer behind him in the terminal. But he was standing opposite a music booth selling pirated CDs, and the song came from inside.

Kid went in. 'What's that?' he said.

'That's paranda,' said the boy behind the till.

'No, but who's singing?' Kid said.

'That's Paul Nabor.'

There are some things you never forget. Your first banana milkshake. Your first kiss. The first time you got drunk. And Kid would never forget the first time he heard paranda being played, beating out the rhythm of Belize, or that most singular of singers, that magician of music, Paul Nabor, electrifying him with the wistful beauty of his voice.

Kid closed his eyes to hide the feeling welling up

in him. Suddenly a music shop in downtown Dangriga was transformed into something close to Paradise. The singer's voice was full of birds and beasts and tall white stately ceiba trees. Flowers were in his voice, and clouds of butterflies, and Kid could hear rivers flowing through the booth, and hear people too. He could hear their voices caught up in the song, and he didn't feel lonely any more. He didn't feel despairing. It didn't matter about not making it to Belmopan. Didn't matter that the day hadn't worked out as planned.

Afterwards, Kid went outside, found a pay phone and dug out his card. No way was he going to get through to the Prime Minister of Belize but at least, when Renata asked, he could say he'd tried, and that might go some way towards redeeming him in her eyes. He tapped in the code on the card and waited to be cut off as a nuisance caller the moment he asked to speak to Mr Dean Barrow. Nothing prepared him for the operator's responding with a quiet and efficient, 'Hold the line. I'm putting you through,' as if phoning the Prime Minister was something that anyone could do.

In the end, Kid didn't get the Right Honourable Dean Barrow, Prime Minister of Belize in person. But he did get his wife at their official residence. Her husband would be back later, Mrs Barrow said as if it was perfectly normal to be rung up by stunned British teenagers in need of advice.

'He's at work just now,' she said. 'But perhaps I could help?'

Afterwards, Kid convinced himself that he'd dreamed the whole thing up, either that or he'd definitely been drugged. But, if so, where did the information come from that the government department dealing with Kekchi-Mayan affairs was based down in Toledo District, in the town of Punta Gorda, not Belmopan?

Kid stumbled out of the phone booth. Parked right in front of him was a pick-up truck full of old men. They pointed at his T-shirt, which bore the Wide-World logo, and one of them said, 'We like yu boys an girls. Yu doin' great tings fi Belize. Where yu goin'? Yu wanna ride?'

Again, paradise.

A couple of days later, having returned to Blue Bank Springs and recovered from the biggest hangover of his life, Kid took the early-morning market bus to Punta Gorda. The rains had stopped at last, the sky was clear and the pretty coastal town on the Gulf of Honduras shimmered in the heat.

Kid could have spent hours exploring the market which, like the one in San Ignacio, was full of clothes, exotic fruit, Mayan wares and Guatemalan weaving. A morning spent mooching along the waterfront wouldn't have gone amiss either, looking at boats on the smooth expanse of silvery-blue sea. But Kid was determined to be disciplined. No messing about this time. No getting side-tracked. Apart from phoning Craig with a progress report on how he was settling in – and getting an earful for not having done so sooner – he cracked straight on with the job in hand.

Finding the government office though, proved more difficult than Kid had expected. Punta Gorda – or PG as all the local people called it – might only be a small town, but the right government department seemed impossible to locate. Kid went through from one side of the town to the other and back again, asking for directions in shops and on the street, only to be told something different by everyone he met.

Finally, however, he succeeded in tracking down an airless office where the air-conditioning had broken down and the sign outside the door had long-since been hidden by bougainvillea. Here a sleepy-looking official handed over a stack of forms and explained what needed to be done with them, where they had to be filled in, what figures might be involved and what supporting documentation would need to be brought back if Blue Bank

Springs wanted a government grant.

Kid left the office in a daze, his head ringing with advice, the last of which had been, 'This is Belize. It's going to take a long time.' But at least one office had done it. At least he didn't have to go anywhere else.

Back on the bus home, an ancient-looking little Mayan woman came and parked herself next to Kid, balancing a massive bundle on her lap. Kid guessed she must have been in the market, selling her wares. Her toothless face was crumpled into hundreds of lines. He reckoned he'd never seen anyone so old before but, astonishingly, her long hair was black with almost no grey in it.

Kid slept for most of the journey, and so did the old woman. But when the bus reached Blue Bank Springs, she awoke and said something in Kekchi-Mayan, poking Kid in the ribs to wake him up as well.

Kid stumbled to his feet, not at first realising where he was. The old woman pushed past him and headed up the bus. It had almost pulled away before Kid had the sense to follow her. He stood on the side of the road, blinking sleep out of his eyes, thinking he was becoming thoroughly Belizean in his ability to drop off anywhere. The old woman said some-thing again in Kekchi-Mayan, and thrust her bundle at Kid as if he was some errant grandchild who didn't know his manners.

Kid carried it up the bank into the village while the old woman waddled ahead on bare feet, snapping at Kid any time he dared walk ahead of her. Kid felt like the browbeaten retainer of some ancient monarch. Halfway up the bank, Renata saw them and rushed down to greet them, followed by Renaldo who wasn't crying *was-yur-name* this time, but 'Xa-an, Xa-an, Xa-an . . .'

Kid was ignored in the rush to reach the old woman and lead her into the house, make her comfortable in the best hammock and slash open a coconut to provide her with a refreshing drink. He and his hurricane shelter grant forms were totally upstaged. The old woman rocked back and forth, her eyes like dots of coal, her smile stretching like a rubber band across her face, talking in Kekchi-Mayan and refusing to stop.

She wasn't just the family's grandmother, Renata explained. She was her and Reuben's mother's grandmother, or maybe even their grandmother's mother – she couldn't quite remember because the old woman went back so many generations that people had lost count.

'Some say that Xa-an is the oldest woman not just in the Mayan villages of Toledo District, but the whole of Belize,' said Renata. 'But certainly she's the wisest, as you'll soon find out. No one could spend time with Xa-an and not realise that. She knows things that everybody else has forgotten about. In fact, there's nothing she doesn't know, so you'd better watch out.'

27

THE SWEAT-HOUSE

That evening Xa-an's arrival was celebrated with a feast of armadillo followed by mugs of *lub*.

Nobody else seemed to have a problem afterwards, but Kid was up half the night, sharing the long-drop with a black, hairy tarantula, too sick to care if it dropped on his head.

Next day, Lydia was mortified to find out that her English guest had been sick, and blamed her cooking. But Renata blamed the armadillo, which Reuben had found dead on the track, and Xa-an informed them that it was nothing to do with what Kid had eaten, but a portent of things to come.

A shadow hung over Kid after that. It was as if Xa-an had spoken something into life. He rocked in his hammock, feeling doom-laden and weak. Across the room he could hear Xa-an still talking, and he wished she'd go back to her own village and take her portents with her.

Kid watched all day as the old woman received visitors as if she really was a royal guest. Her lips were so cracked that they scarcely seemed to move, and her thin, rasping voice seemed to rise up from her chest. But however she managed it, the words kept coming. On one occasion, she started crying, and Kid had no idea why. On another occasion great cackles of laughter broke out of her like flames from a log.

Renata said later that Xa-an had come to tell them of some family member in her village who had died. She also said there were things Xa-an told people about that they'd only otherwise know from learning them in school. Things in history that she'd seen with her own eyes. Things that would go with her when she died because no one else was left who'd witnessed them.

Even when Kid fell asleep that night, Xa-an was still holding court, which meant it wasn't until the following morning, while she was still asleep, that he had the chance to tell Reuben how he'd got on in Punta Gorda. Reuben said he'd done a great job and should feel proud of himself. It was a Sunday morning – Reuben's day off from the sawmill – and he was heading off to farm his land on the other side of the river. Did Kid want to come with him, he asked, and see if he had in him the makings of a farmer?

It felt like a reward, and Kid was honoured to be invited. He was pleased to make himself useful and pleased, too, to get away from Xa-an and her court. The two of them set off across the river, fording it at the shallowest point. But Kid had only just arrived when he went all clammy and started shivering. Was his sickness coming back? He hoped to God it wasn't. He tried all day to hide how he was feeling and somehow succeeded, even managing at times to drive the shivers away. But, in the early hours of the next morning, he awoke with a burning headache and a full-scale fever.

Kid tried fixing it with pills from his med-kit, but they made no difference. For the rest of the night, he either poured with sweat or shivered with violent rigors. By morning, when Reuben got up for work, Kid could scarcely speak.

'I th-th-think . . . I m-m-mean . . . I m-m-might . . .'

Reuben called for Lydia. The two of them looked down at Kid, their faces swimming before his eyes. Renata's face appeared as well, and then Renaldo's. Then Lydia's mother, Selina, was there as well, and so were half her friends, for some reason, all shaking their heads.

Finally Xa-an joined them, looking down at Kid as if she'd seen it all before. No doubt at her great age, Kid thought, one sick boy looked very much like any other.

'D-d-doctor . . .' he whispered, mustering all his energy for one single coherent word.

But if a doctor came, he never knew about it. For the rest of the day, Kid was out of things and knew very little. Occasionally he sensed people close by, but he was never sure if they were real or if he was imagining them. In his rare lucid moments, he tried remembering what he'd learned about tropical diseases, courtesy of Cassie and Doc Rose. Malaria was contracted from mosquitoes, if he remembered rightly, and there were plenty of those here in Blue Bank Springs, and had he taken all his malaria pills – he couldn't remember. But dengue fever was meant to be just as bad, if not worse. Then there was cholera to worry about, followed by rabies, hepatitis and even yellow fever which, if Kid remembered right, he wasn't supposed to catch in Belize . . .

Kid's mind rambled on. He pictured his body being flown home with a Union Jack draped over it. Was this real, he asked himself? Was he imagining it or was it an actual out-of-body experience? The plane touched down outside Jet's Burger Bar, and Jet wasn't there to greet him, and neither was Nadine – though no surprises there. But Snow was there, dressed in black, followed by Jez who was weeping like a girl and Cassie who kept repeating, over and over, *I told him to be careful.*

It was the start of a night of wild imaginings. Faces hung over Kid, some friendly, some downright scary. At one point, Kid imagined Jack-the-Goth standing over his grave, dressed in a black leather trench-coat, his hair dyed blue, carrying a cross. Then *brujos* visited his night – snakes and scorpions with human faces and black human hearts. And there were voices too. Voices from Kid's past.

Desperately Kid tried telling himself that he was safe now – that all the bad things in his life lay in the past, and he wasn't back in south London, he was still in Belize. But, if so, why could Kid hear his mother calling out for him? And why could he hear her friends and half-friends, relatives and cousins once-removed all arguing over who would have to take him?

These people were meant to be in England, but Kid could feel their presence in the darkness. They were here in Blue Bank Springs, here in this house. Their voices went on and on but none of them spoke to him.

Kid cried out. He struggled to get out of his hammock but hands were holding him down. Where they'd come from he'd no idea, but Kid wasn't a boy to be held down. He fought against them with his

whole strength. People kept telling him to stay still –
but it wasn't until the sudden smell of incense filled
the room that he gave up his struggle and calmed
down.

What was happening now? Had his body been
moved? Was it in church or something? Was he –
God forbid – *was he waiting for his own funeral?*

A still small voice whispered in Kid's ear. He'd be
all right, his mother said, he'd be all right. He fell
asleep. When he opened his eyes again, the smell of
incense was still there but her voice had gone, and
so had everybody else's. Kid whimpered like a baby
waking from a nap. Immediately Renata was on one
side of him and Lydia on the other.

'What's happened to me?' Kid whispered.

'Something's bitten you,' Lydia said. 'That's what
Xa-an says. You have poisoned blood, she says, and
she's going to help you sweat it out.'

The thought of any more sweating made Kid feel
weak. 'I can't . . .' he whispered.

'Can't what?' said Lydia.

'Can't anything . . .' whispered Kid – and fell back
to sleep.

Next time he came round, Kid was outside being
carried through the heat of the day. People were all
around him, but where were they taking him?
Dimly Kid was aware of the village passing by and

the river coming into view. Trees hung over him, and he was on some part of the riverbank where he'd never been before. A rough-hewn stone building stood in front of him, about the size of a child's play-house. Smoke was seeping out through its cracks. Its door was open and he could see the glowing embers of a fire inside.

What was going on? Kid didn't know. Dimly he was aware that he wasn't wearing any clothes. There was nothing dim, however, about the moment he was slid into the little house like a loaf into a bread oven. He struggled to get out, but wasn't strong enough. Through the blinding heat, he was aware of somebody directing his body and moving him about. Then a door closed behind them both, daylight disappearing as if snuffed out, and even the sounds outside seemed to be snuffed out.

And then the heat started building up.

Kid lay on the ground feeling himself cook. Breathing was an effort and the heat was so intense that it peeled back his eyes. Not only that, but if sweat was required of him, he was already exceeding expectations.

Kid poured with sweat. It ran off him in rivulets. Steam filled the air around him, and Kid heard the hiss of water being poured on to hot stones. His sense of confinement was overwhelming. He started panicking, but someone splashed the walls with incense and it worked again to calm him down, just as it had done before.

Kid breathed in. The incense was the perfume of his dreams. He closed his eyes and drifted away. His body was no longer his own, and neither was his mind. Dimly he was aware of someone taking up a bundle of herbs and beating him. Their perfume mingled with the incense and filled his head. Then he heard water being poured on stones again, and wood piled on to the fire.

Once or twice the door was opened to call for the water jar to be filled, or more firewood sent in. But, by now, Kid had lost all sense of time. He was aware of steam being directed on to his body as he drifted in and out of consciousness, and aware of being beaten by the herbs. Once he was even aware of the jar of incense being held directly under his nose. And once he was forced to drink something which tasted bitter but he swallowed it all down.

But, apart from that, the rest was a dream.

It took until nightfall for the stones to cool down. By now the fire had burned out and the door had been opened wide enough for Kid to see the world outside. He felt a mat of woven grasses being slid under him, then hands taking hold of its corners and lifting him out. The evening that greeted him was clear and fresh. Stars stood above him in the sky and a small handful of people – not half the village this time, but just Lydia, Renata, Reuben and Xa-an – stood over him as if waiting for some final thing to happen.

Kid lay before them all, too tired to care what it might be, knowing he was naked but not caring about that either. Xa-an took a step towards him. From her ringing wet hair and sodden dress, Kid realised she'd been the one in the sweat-house with him, whipping him with bunches of herbs, forcing him to swallow that vile drink, feeding the fire, feeding the steam, nursing him all day.

And now she was the one who spoke to him in Kekchi-Mayan – and Kid understood. How did she do that? *He understood!*

Renata started translating, but it wasn't necessary. Already Kid was on his feet, staggering towards the river, attempting to do what Xa-an had bidden:

'For your cure to be complete, you need to bathe. Only when the river has soaked into your body will your blood be cleansed and the burning heat be cast out of your bones.'

Kid didn't need to be told twice. Finding a strength within himself that he didn't know he had, he waded into the cool water and let it carry him downstream. Then slowly he started swimming back, gaining strength with every stroke. The river seemed to caress him. He felt it soaking into him. He was enveloped in freshness. He felt safe. And, more than safe, he felt alive.

Even more than at Natural Arch, when he'd unburdened himself to Jez about his past, Kid knew this was the swim of his life. He remained in the water for a long time, not wanting it to end. When he did finally wade out, he found the riverbank empty. Even Xa-an had gone. Clean clothes had been left for him, but Kid stood alone.

He dressed slowly, cool-bodied and clear-headed, savouring how good it was to be restored to health. Then he walked back through the village, taking stock of everything around him. Fireflies danced in the air. Smoke rose from thatches and melted into the darkness. The distant Maya Mountains, lit by the moon, looked as if they were covered in snow.

The world was beautiful. For days Kid had been too sick to see it, but now he could. That's what being healed was all about.

28

RENATA

Next day Kid tried to make himself useful by filling in forms. His desire to give something back to a village that had fed, nurtured and now even healed him was greater than ever. He even talked about going back to the school, pleading with Teacher Betty to give him another chance.

Xa-an, however, insisted that he wasn't ready. Maybe Kid felt better, she said, but there was a difference between feeling better and returning to one's life. For the next few days, she watched Kid like a hawk, taking on the role of nurse and supervising what he ate. Renata was her assistant, dancing in attendance as if being trained up. In particular, she was put in charge of keeping at bay the endless stream of visitors who wanted to see the miraculously healed boy.

Everybody wanted to touch Kid, as if his good

health might rub off on them, and to congratulate Xa-an who had proved – as if any proof was necessary – the wisdom of her years. Blue Bank Springs was enveloped in an atmosphere of celebration. Lydia was delighted to show off her guest, but Xan-an had spoken and Renata wouldn't be budged.

On the third day, however, after keeping Kid indoors the whole while, Renata announced that she had something to show Kid, and took him off into the forest. Every day, Renata said, even before the rest of them had known that Kid was sick and would be in need of a cure, Xa-an had been to the copal tree collecting sap. They stood before it now and Renata explained that first Xa-an had prayed in church for the tree to give it up. She'd prayed to the Virgin Mary, and her prayers had been answered – either that or the *Duende* had heard her, because never had a tree given up so much sweet-smelling incense in such a short time.

This sounded different to any religion Kid had ever come across before. He said something about trees as givers of life, and Renata agreed.

Trees were all about giving, she said. Each had something to offer, even if some didn't look as if they did. Take this spiky tree, for example, which everybody called the 'give and take' – its spikes were used for darts but its leaves provided healing. Then here was the allspice tree, whose leaves smelt good enough to eat. Then here was the sapodilla, whose milky *chicle* went in to making chewing gum. And here was the coco plum, not only good to eat, but excellent for extracting oil to make candles.

Renata moved with ease through the forest, naming everything she touched. Kid was impressed. She certainly knew her plants and shrubs, he said. Renata replied that so she should because trees and Mayan people went back a long way.

'Once this forest garden was known by our people's name,' she said. 'It was called the Maya Forest, but then the people disappeared and then the forest started disappearing, too. Logging companies moved in. Trees started coming down. Citrus walks replaced jungle. Roads started going up.'

They walked back towards the village, Renata pointing out things all the way. Breadfruit, poisonwood, gumbolimbo, frangipani, hibiscus and finally the black orchid, Belize's national flower – she knew them all. Kid felt like a voyager being carried along on a vast green sea. Only when Renata asked about England's trees, and he couldn't name a single one apart from oak, did he finally come in to land.

'I'm a London boy myself,' he said. 'Where I live there aren't any trees.'

Renata was astonished. She couldn't imagine a

place where there weren't any trees. Kid could have corrected himself, explaining there were *some* trees but he didn't know their names. But it was nice having Renata's sympathy.

She wanted to know all about England after that. But England was boring, Kid said. Why didn't they talk about something else?'

'Like what?' Renata said.

'Well, like you,' Kid said. 'Why you're always smiling, even when you're tired. And why your face shines even when it isn't smiling. That's a mystery I'd like to solve.'

Renata blushed at that. She blushed like a woman being paid a compliment by a man, and then Kid felt himself blushing too because it was a soppy, thoroughly wet thing to have said. But, even so, Renata's face did shine. It shone all the time and there was a gracefulness about her – an air of confidence that made her stand out.

Perhaps it was to do with living in a forest that had once been named after her people, in full view of mountains that had been named after them too. But there was a rootedness about Renata, a sense of belonging that made her beautiful, and Kid wished he could be rooted too.

He, on the other hand, was always on the move. Always heading for somewhere new. That's what life had been like back in London, sofa-surfing as a way of life. And it had been the same here, hopping restlessly from one place to the next.

Renata, however, had been born here in this forest garden whose trees she knew by name, and she would die here one day.

'You never tell me about yourself,' Kid said. 'You always talk about other things. I want to know about you.'

Renata looked puzzled, as if she didn't know what to say. But, before supper that night, she dug out the family scrapbook full of black-and-white photographs, and the two of them sat on the bench outside and looked at them. This was her as a baby in her mother's arms, and this was her on Reuben and Lydia's wedding day and here she was in her white dress on the day the bishop came to Blue Bank Springs for her to be confirmed. And here she was, holding Renaldo when he was born.

Finally Renata finished, closing the book as if to say *now you know it all*. The sun had set by now, and the first few stars were coming out. Kid had never seen so many of them, and never so bright. He asked Renata for their names in Mayan. But, unlike the trees, she didn't know them.

Lydia called them in to eat. There were hot tortillas steaming under their cloth, and rice and beans with a lump of meat on top which Lydia said was gibnut. After they'd finished eating, the only argument Kid ever heard in Blue Bank Springs suddenly blew up. It was between Xa-an and Reuben, and conducted in Kekchi-Mayan, which Kid no longer understood because the moment of enlightenment by the river had gone and Renata had to translate.

Xa-an, apparently, was saying that once the Maya had been powerful warlords, and they could be powerful again. There were people, she had heard, who wanted all the Mayan people in the Americas to rise up and fight for their rights.

Reuben, however, said, 'We Kekchi aren't just Mayans, we're Belizeans too. All we people in this country – Garifuna, Creoles, Mestizos, British, Americans, even Taiwanese – if each forgets the others and fights for its own rights, that's the end of Belize.'

The patriotism left Kid cold, but the simplicity of Reuben's argument really got to him, and so did its sheer unselfishness. Reuben might have few rights by many people's standards, but a longing washed over Kid that his life might be like his.

Lydia broke up the argument, saying that Reuben and Xa-an were too alike. They both talked too much and should retire to bed. When they'd done just that, however, Renata confided to Kid that she stood by every word her brother had said. He was a wise man, she said. One day, after Joseph, he'd be Alcalde. Anyone with any sense could see that.

Kid said some people might think loyalty to country over personal gain was a crazy way of living one's life. But Renata said the way they lived made perfect sense to her.

'Everybody here in Blue Bank Springs helps everybody else,' she said. 'It's our way. The *fajina* way, we call it. For the good of all. And Reuben reckons that what's good for Blue Bank Springs could one day be good for the whole of Belize. He thinks the country needs a different way of governing and could learn a lot from the Kekchi-Mayan people. He thinks about these things. Like the problem of the land. He thinks about that, too.'

There were no problems that Kid could see. He asked Renata what she meant, and she explained that the land wasn't theirs.

'But the government gave it to Joseph,' Kid said.

'No they didn't. Not the title deeds. What they gave was permission to settle,' Renata said.

Kid was shocked. What would happen, he asked, if oil men from Texas found reserves beneath the ground? Or if gold was found or if, once the paved roads had gone through, the government decided to build houses and hotels? Renata's eyes burned when

Kid said that. If she was Alcalde, she said she'd give her life to making sure that none of those things happened. And her brother would do the same. But everybody's hopes were pinned on the new government looking after the Kekchi-Mayan people, so that such terrible things would never happen.

Kid could have said that, where he came from, trusting politicians was generally seen to be a mistake. But he bit his tongue. After all, what did he know about anything? Maybe things were different in Belize. Certainly they'd been different when it came to phoning Prime Ministers and their wives. Maybe in Belize there really were politicians who were honest, and people's hopes weren't always misplaced.

Kid envied them their hope. That night he went to bed half in love with a way of looking at the world that felt out of reach. And from there it was a short way to falling in love properly. On the other side of the room, Renata lay curled up on her mat with a cover thrown over her. She was a proper, grown-up woman, but Kid was just a boy – which meant she'd never give him a second thought.

But all the same, Kid was in love.

29

BURNING

Next morning Kid awoke knowing that everything he could possibly want in life was here in Blue Bank Springs. He imagined being man enough to build his own house, tend his own farm and come home at night to his own wife. The picture stayed with him all day. Even going to school and attempting to make himself useful made no difference. Wisely Teacher Betty put him in charge of the football team instead of allowing him back in the classroom. But even dashing up and down in the hot sun, Kid couldn't stop thinking about Renata and the home he'd make with her, if only he was old enough for her to look his way.

At the end of the day, drained of hope as well as energy, Kid headed home. Teacher Betty walked along with him, heading for her bus. She'd been in a mood all day, rapping pupils with her sharp tongue and threatening to do the same with her ruler if they didn't pull themselves together. Now she huffed and puffed as she walked along. Plainly something was on her mind. And, being Teacher Betty, it wasn't long before it came bursting out.

'Bright children like dese. Dey could become lawyers if dey had yur chances. Dey could become doctors. Dey could become teachers like me. Dey have brains an' dere keen. It isn't fair. Yu English boys an' gyals, yu have it all. Dere's a gyal in my class – a lovely gyal, real shiny an' sharp. She sat de exam to go to school in Punta Gorda instead of leavin' at fourteen. An' she passed de exam. She got top marks. But her mudder's jus' been in to say she can't take up de place.

'De school is proud of her,' Teacher Betty fumed. 'Her family's proud of her. Everybody's proud of her. She's even proud of herself. But pride's one ting an' money's another and de gyal can't go. She's grateful fo de chance. But it mek no difference. When de new term starts dat gyal won' be there.'

They'd reached the road now and stood together waiting for Teacher Betty's bus. Kid said something about people here being happy all the same, and Teacher Betty snorted.

'Of course dey's happy,' she said, giving Kid a sour look. 'Dey always are, dese people. But it doesn't mean dat tings are right. Take yur Renata. She was de same. We went through this whole ting a year ago. Now she's fifteen an' helping to look after her brudder's family when she coulda gone away to school. An' is she unhappy? Of course she's not – she's a proud Kekchi-Mayan girl. But *I'm* unhappy. I, Teacher Betty. I see de way de world works. I see de way it's stacked. *An' I know it ain't fair.'*

Kid blushed when Teacher Betty said that. He thought of his own schooling record – all the chances he'd let slip by, the classes he'd missed, the exams he'd skived. Even now while he was here in Belize, his classmates in England would be sweating over their GCSEs. Kid's whole life was one massive skive.

The bus came along and Teacher Betty boarded it. Kid waved her off, then turned for home. The argument was more complicated than Teacher Betty made out, but then he guessed she knew it wasn't just an education that was being weighed in the balance here. It was a way of life – a choice between the world Teacher Betty came from, and Kid as well, with its pockets full of money and big-deal careers, or a world where, if you wanted a fish, you went and caught it; if you wanted fruit you picked it off the tree.

Kid headed up the bank. Ahead of him he could

see Renaldo on a turkey, riding it in circles, Lydia on the sewing-machine and Renata taking in a line of washing. He watched her unpegging it item by item, folding it and placing it in her basket. And suddenly something Teacher Betty had said finally sank in.

How old was Renata?

Kid stopped in his tracks. 'What are you staring at?' Renata said, looking up.

Kid didn't ask then. He saved it until later, and worked his way round to it by asking Reuben first. 'I was just wondering,' he said. 'I hope you don't mind asking, but how old are you?'

Reuben said he was twenty – the same age as Hal. Lydia, he said, a mother of two children, was nineteen, the same age as Snow and Fritz. And Renata –

'Renata is fifteen,' he said.

'*Fifteen?*' said Kid, unable to disguise the thrill that ran through him.

Reuben smiled as if he understood that Kid might be shocked. 'Our world's not like yours,' he said. 'In our world, a woman of fifteen is old enough to marry, and a man of sixteen – like I was at the time – old enough to build a house and become a father.'

After that, Kid looked at Renata in a whole new light. Looked at himself in a new light too, for boys his age were capable of things he'd never have thought possible. He waited until the others had gone to bed, then fished out his parents' photograph and told Renata all about them. It was as if he wanted her to know who he really was. He told her his father's name and explained about looking for him but said he'd found out in the end that he was dead. Maybe it wasn't quite true, but Kid reckoned it was near enough.

'In fact, both my parents are dead,' he said. 'Just like yours.'

It was as if he was trying to forge a connection with Renata. As if he wanted to say *look, we're both the same*.

Renata asked about his mother and he said her name was Kath, and showed Renata her hat. She said she loved it, and she looked great in it when she tried it on. Kid was almost tempted to give it to her. He could sense something in her that hadn't been there before. Thanks to one white lie – which was probably more truth than lie anyway – a bond was struck between them. Renata viewed him differently now. Kid could sense the shift in her.

That night, he couldn't sleep. The thought of Renata across the room, no longer out of touch, but within grasp, was too much to bear. Kid imagined her awake, thinking of him too. He even went so far as to imagine her tiptoeing across the floor and sneaking into his hammock to keep him company. He knew it wasn't going to happen, not least because this was the same Renata who'd found no one yet who measured up to her brother. But it was nice imagining it.

Kid had never been in love. Never even thought he was in love, though there'd been girls he'd fancied who had fancied him back. He'd certainly never imagined wanting to get married and settle down. But he was imagining it now. Teacher Betty had misunderstood these Kekchi-Mayan people, he thought. She hadn't got the measure of their lives. This mightn't be a place where you could become a doctor or lawyer. But it was one where you could become a man.

Kid lay in his hammock dreaming about living in the village as Renata's husband, surrounded by their children, even becoming Alcalde himself one day, everybody looking up to him and coming to him for advice.

But how to make it happen? That was the thing. Kid knew nothing about how Kekchi-Mayan courtships were conducted but guessed, like anywhere else, that the first thing was to declare his love.

Next morning, Kid arose with a sense of purpose. It was Saturday, which meant that the village children were all off school, which in turn meant that finding a moment alone with Renata was going to be difficult. Kid watched her every move. He was determined to seize his chance when it came along. He waited half the morning, thinking it never would, but finally Renata picked up a basket of washing and headed off towards the river.

Kid trailed behind, rehearsing what he'd say when his chance presented itself. But voices came his way as he drew closer to the river. And by the time he stood on the ridge looking down upon the water, it seemed as if half the village women were there.

Kid had never been to the river before when the women were washing. They were all in the water, some right up to their waists, and the sight of their brightly coloured dresses spread out around them like beautiful flowers was one he'd never forget. He watched them pounding mounds of soapy washing on a series of flat stones, worn smooth by use. Children splashed around them and babies wrapped in tight bundles, hung like ripe fruit in the trees.

Kid stood mesmerised. A few of the women pulled off their dresses to wash them too, and he knew that he should look away. But Renata stood amongst them unplaiting her hair, and it was the first time Kid had seen it loose. He stood watching like a peeping tom, astonished at how long it was. Then Renata pulled off her dress too, and Kid *really* should have looked away, but he couldn't do it. He stood burning up instead.

After that, Kid burned all day. He'd succeeded in finally dragging himself away, but the picture of Renata standing in the river still filled his head. He knew he couldn't carry on like this. He had to do something. He had to share his feelings. He wished that Fritz or Hal were here, or even Snow. He hadn't missed them until now, but suddenly he missed them terribly. They'd understand the way he felt. Better still, they'd give him good advice.

Kid filled the day somehow, one minute sticking to Renata and trying to drop hints, the next sloping off miserably when she didn't pick them up. Finally he decided that if Renata didn't have the time to hear what he had to say, he'd explain his love to Lydia and ask for her advice.

Before he could explain anything, however, Renata came out of the house looking for him. 'There's a visitor inside for you,' she said.

'What, *me*?' Kid said.

'Yes, you,' Renata said.

There was something in her expression that Kid couldn't quite figure out. Something in her tone as well. Kid followed her back to the house, where she stepped aside to let him in. In the dim light he saw a man lounging in one of the hammocks. He stood up when Kid appeared – a tall stranger wearing a grey vest, pin-striped trousers held up with braces, flip-flop sandals and a baseball cap.

Kid squinted to see more clearly. The man stepped forward and Kid made out eyes the colour of amber, a face which marked the man out as a Creole and one other distinguishing feature, in that the man looked just like him.

An older version maybe, but he had Kid's face.

The man stared at Kid and Kid stared back. For a moment neither of them spoke, then the man said, in a rumbling voice, 'Well, looks like Ai ended up in de right village den.'

He stuck out his hand. Kid stared at it. 'You're not . . .' he said, and broke off.

The man replied. 'Ai am,' he said. 'You got dat right. Ai's de one yu been lookin' for. An' you must be mah boy.'

30

CATO & SON

Kid's father took him in his arms. His long-lost father picked him up and gave him a back-slapping, monumental bear-hug. It was one way, Kid supposed, of greeting a son you'd never met. He extracted himself, not knowing what he should do or say. Dimly, he was aware of Renata standing in the doorway watching them, her eyes accusing him of having lied to her about his father being dead.

It was over, wasn't it? No girl wanted a man who lied to her. Kid had wanted to find his father, but not like this, and definitely not just now. The timing couldn't have been worse. The thing with Renata was over before it ever started, and the thing with Blue Bank Springs as well.

Renaldo came hurtling into the house, delighted that yet another stranger had decided to turn up. He flung himself at the older version of Kid, knocked off his baseball cap and cried out, 'Was-yur-name?'

Kid's father laughed, stooped down and swung Renaldo up in the air. He liked little kids, he said, completely unabashed before the son he'd abandoned when he was a little kid himself.

Kid bit his tongue. Now wasn't the moment for bitterness, he told himself. This was the father he'd come all this way to find. He watched in dumb amazement as Renaldo worked his way up on to the stranger's shoulders and started pulling his hair.

'Was-yur-name?' he asked again, and Kid's father introduced himself as Marcus Aurelius Cato, adding, 'But Cato's good nuff name fu mi. Plain ol' Cato – dat's what pipple call me.'

It was Cato after that. Kid's father never said to call him 'Dad', and Kid wouldn't have done so anyway. Not knowing what else to do with a father he'd never met before, he took him on an excursion of the village, accompanied by a procession of children. His father declared himself enchanted with everything he saw, but Kid couldn't figure out whether he meant it or not. This man was an unknown quantity. They might be related – might even have the same face. But Kid didn't know the first thing about him.

And Cato didn't appear about to enlighten him. He asked plenty of questions, both about the village and about Kid, wanting to know what he was doing here, why he'd come, what he thought of Belize and even how much money he had, and whether he kept it on him or in the bank. But in return he gave nothing away, not on the subject of how he'd got here and, even more so, not on why he'd come. Kid felt confused and disoriented. This wasn't what finding his father was meant to be like, and it definitely wasn't how his day was meant to end up.

'How did you find me?' he demanded to know.

Cato looked cagey. He said that Wide-World Treks had given him Kid's address. Kid didn't know whether to believe him. Something here just didn't add up.

'How did you know about Wide-World Treks?' he asked.

Cato shrugged. Again the cagey look. He'd looked for Kid round the bars of San Ignacio, he said and Craig's name had come up.

'But why San Ignacio?' Kid persisted. 'Why there, of all places? And why were you looking for me, anyway? How did you know I was even in Belize?'

By this time, Cato actually had the grace to look abashed. 'Yu sure is full of questions,' he said. 'Well, Ai's a brave man, so Ai tell you alla 'bout it, maan to maan. Tell yu de truth, Ai's de one who fix dat note sending yu to Cayo. Ai tried to mek yu go away, if yu muss know. Ai sent yu on a false trail so yu wouldn't track mi down. Ai didn't want a son, to mi great shame. But now Ai do. Ai got to tinking, and so here Ai am.'

Kid digested this piece of information. His father stood before him like a guilty child hoping for forgiveness, but Kid felt too betrayed for anything like that. He thought of all the places the lies in his father's note had led him, and the terrible things that could have happened. That they hadn't was no thanks to the man before him now. And yet here he stood, hoping to be told that now he and his son had found each other nothing else mattered.

'How did you know I was even looking for you?' Kid demanded in a cold, angry voice.

Cato flashed a dazzling smile at him. That was obvious, he said. 'Yu tink a boy wid mi face could walk through Belize City widout word gettin' back?' he said. 'All Belize City knows Marcus Aurelius Cato. Ai's a famous city resident.'

Kid remembered the Sisters of Jesus woman who'd tried to save his soul. *She* hadn't known his father, he said, and neither had the people at the hotel. Neither had the people in the music store, nor the ones in the supermarket.

'You're not as famous as you think,' he said.

Cato laughed. 'Dose pipple was tryin' to protect

yu,' he said. 'Of course dey knew mi. Dey was try-ing to mek yu go away.'

'And why would they do that?'

'Bikaaz yur daddy used to be a bad man,' Cato said. 'But not any more. Mi ways are mended. Ai have a son. Ai am reformed.'

Reformed or not, that evening after supper a con-versation sprang up between Cato and Reuben about land. The two men sat outside, looking across the village towards the mountains. Cato told Reuben 'maan to maan' that he had a nice place here, which could be worth a bit, and offered his services as an honest broker if he ever wanted to sell his land. The whole transaction was priced, right down to Cato's cut, before Reuben could even explain that he didn't own the land.

'Not dat Ai's takin' advantage,' Cato hastened to reassure. 'Ai's de Top Director of one of de coun-try's major land agency development tings. Ai has framed qualificashuns on mi office wall. Yu can come and see dem any time. In addition, dis boy of mine is comin' in wid me, which means you always have access to de top man. So if mi offer is of inter-est . . .'

He got no further. Kid, who'd been sitting at some distance, head in hands, feeling as if his whole world had come crashing in on him, looked up and said, 'This boy of yours is doing *what*?'

Cato gestured him over. A unique opportunity to make something of himself was being offered here, he said, and all because Kid was his son. Any other boy would die for a chance like this. But it was Kid's for the taking.

'Cato an' Son,' he said. 'Yu an' yur daddy – wha' yu tink?'

Kid thought his father was a crook. At least that's what he said later, when he finally had the chance to talk to Renata. All this time he'd longed to find his father, he said, and had dreamt about what he'd be like. He'd hoped to find a father to be proud of, despite certain things his mother had said, but the father who'd turned up totally shamed him.

'But then I feel ashamed anyway,' Kid admitted, 'for lying to you. I didn't mean to do it. I'm really, really sorry.'

Maybe that was a lie too, but Renata forgave him for it. She didn't forgive him, though, for saying his father shamed him.

'Maybe he's not the father you imagined,' she said. 'But he wants the same as any father – for his son to be proud of him.'

'How can I be proud of a person like that?'

'By getting to know him.'

'And how do I do that?'

'It's obvious. Go home with him. He's come all the way from Belize City to find you. Now's your chance to do something for him.'

For the second time that day, Kid felt betrayed. This was the girl he was in love with, yet she was trying to get rid of him.

'How can you say that?' he said. 'Everything I want is here. Renata, look at me. You know exactly what I'm talking about . . .'

Renata looked at him, but her face wasn't shining like it usually did, and her eyes were grave.

'Life here's not as easy as you might think,' she said. 'I know you want to stay. I see you dreaming. But we Kekchi people have hard lives. This is no Paradise, like you seem to think. So, go with your father. It means a lot to him. He's your father, after all. Find out about his life. And think about the life for you. Then maybe one day you'll return. But not like this. When you can see clearly, come back then. And, if you can't, *better stay away.*'

Part Six

Caye Caulker

31

BELIZE CITY BLUES

Kid couldn't sleep that night. For hours he lay awake thinking about what Renata had said. With nothing else to do, he pulled out a letter his father had given him forwarded by the Wide-World people, apparently, and read it by candlelight.

It came from Snow and caught him up on all the news. The bunkhouse was finished now, and people were going their separate ways. Jez was heading off to Papua New Guinea where he'd be leading another Wide-World expedition. Doc Rose was backpacking round South America along with Cassie. A few people, including Sam and Benji, had taken up placements like Kid's and were hoping to look him up. Hubert had finished his tour of duty in the forest and was on border patrol up north, between Belize and Mexico. And most of the rest, including Snow, were on the island of Caye Caulker, diving off the reef on their last few days before heading home.

'I wish that you could join us,' Snow wrote. 'I know you're on your placement but, just in case, this is where we are . . .'

Kid folded up the letter without bothering to read the address. He didn't want to witness the final break-up of the old team, thank you very much. If a curtain was coming down in his life, he didn't want to know about it. The thought of the old camp being empty, its kitchen unused and saplings growing up through its dormitories was more than he could bear.

Next morning, however, when Cato left Blue Bank Springs, taking Kid with him, another curtain came down. It was Sunday, which meant hitching a ride rather than taking the bus. Reuben accompanied them down to the road, to see them off, and Xa-an stood in the doorway with Lydia, Renaldo watching from between their legs. But there was no sign of Renata.

Kid waited half an hour to thumb down a ride, wondering all the time why she didn't come. After all, here he was, following her advice. Finally a truck pulled up and Cato climbed on board, followed by Kid, for what turned out to be their dream lift, heading at breakneck speed, with no stops, all the way to Belize City.

Kid slept for part of the journey and pretended he was sleeping for the rest, because he didn't want to talk. They arrived in the city just in time for the afternoon traffic jam at Haulover Creek when the swing bridge was opened to allow boats up and down. Even though it was Sunday, and the banks and offices were shut, there was still a buzz about the city.

Kid watched water-taxis full of tourists heading out to the cayes on the reef. Beyond them a couple of cruise ships sat in the bay, waiting for their passengers to return from shore. The area around the swing-bridge was heaving with stalls selling trinkets to tourists with white faces and even whiter T-shirts.

Kid watched them dodging hustlers, clutching their money-belts and plainly terrified of being ripped off. I was one of those, he thought. When I first arrived, that same scared expression was written all over my face as well.

Finally the bridge opened and the traffic started moving again. On the far side of Haulover Creek, Cato called for the driver to drop them off. He ambled off, leaving Kid to thank the driver, then follow him into a mesh of tightly connected back streets lined with what Cato casually referred to as 'upstayz houses'. If he'd been alone, Kid would have immediately been lost. But Cato could have made this journey with his eyes shut. He knew every last broken sidewalk, and everyone he met seemed to be his friend.

'Hey, maan. Hey, Cato. How's tings?' people called. And Cato called back that tings were great. This was his son. They'd be out tonight. See you later, everyone.

Finally they reached Cato's house. Kid had known his father wasn't really a top director in some land agency, and that it wouldn't be the white house of his dreams, but he hadn't expected anything quite so dilapidated. A wooden staircase led to a littered balcony with rotting boards. Slatted wooden shutters hung at the windows, plainly in need of a coat of paint. A door hung on its hinges as if someone had smashed into it. Even the hammock strung across the balcony had holes in it.

'Come on up, son,' Cato said.

Kid followed him upstairs, missing out the broken risers. Together they picked their way across a debris of empty cans and bottles, entering a single room smelling of bottled gas and alcohol. A stove stood in one corner and a bed in the other. Unwashed dishes were stacked in the sink attracting flies in and out through a broken mosquito screen. Cato's clothes were thrown about everywhere and his bed looked as if it was rarely slept in. The hammock on the balcony appeared to be the place where he spent most of his time.

Cato headed for the fridge, grabbed a couple of beers, then headed back outside, saying, 'Mek yu at home.' He flung himself into the hammock, pulling out his mobile phone, and said he had a couple of business calls to make.

Kid was left to his own devices. He leant over the balcony, wondering what exactly he was doing here. It was getting dark now. Cars were out there in the gathering night, squealing on their tyres, music was in the air and there was a police siren wailing somewhere. Blue Bank Springs felt a million miles away.

Cato came off the phone and said he had to go out. He wouldn't be long, he said and, in the meantime, Kid should get dressed. 'We goin' fo big night out. Fader an' son. On de town. We goin' somewhere nice, so dress up smart,' he said.

Kid rummaged through his rucksack and did his best with what he'd got, which wasn't much. Then he went outside and leant over the balcony again. Dogs mooched past the house and people called out. A couple of Cato's friends even came upstairs to make Kid's acquaintance. It didn't need him to be there to say *dis mi son*. They said that they could see it for themselves.

Finally Cato returned, though not in the best of moods. He washed, shaved, ironed a shirt, slapped on some aftershave and then the two of them headed off together. Kid wondered what he was in for. Part of him was filled with trepidation but a small core of excitement was in there somewhere too.

As they walked the streets, Kid heard televisions blaring, music playing, people laughing to each other and calling out from house to house. They reached an area where strings of lights hung between the trees and he could hear the ocean slapping over the sea wall. They were on the edge of the commercial district now, close to the Ocean Hotel. Briefly Kid savoured what it felt like to be a local and not a tourist any more. But being a local didn't feel good when suddenly, without warning, his father turned in to the entrance of an open-air tourist restaurant and started working his way from table to table.

What was he up to? Kid quickly found out. He hung back in embarrassment, but his father pulled him over. He was talking to the tourists at the tables as if they were old friends, cracking jokes, slapping them on the back, trying to persuade someone, anyone, that he and his younger brother here – *his younger brother* – should join them for supper at their expense.

Kid was mortified. His father offered the two of them as some sort of dynamic duo to inject local colour into the tourists' night out. Kid was introduced as the clever one, English-educated, home to join the family firm.

'Ai's de Top Director of one of de country's major land agency development tings,' Cato said. 'Ai's a big maan in Bileez City. Ai can show you a good time.'

Kid blushed and tried to get away. The tourists were distinctly unimpressed. And so was the restaurant manager, who threw them out.

The manager of the next restaurant was equally unsympathetic. Cato tried another tack this time, saying that Kid was his son, home from England for the first time and the honour of the country depended on this, his first night, giving a good impression.

But it made no difference and, after this, the word went round all the other restaurants, which meant that their managers were waiting for them when Cato bowled up. Kid tried to pull his father away, but still Cato kept trying to talk his way in. He was totally unabashed.

Only when somebody threatened to call the police did Cato finally give up. The night ended in a take-away shack, buying a boil-up of sweet potatoes and pigtail, flavoured with coconut oil. Some big night out, Kid thought, ignoring his father's apologies. If he hadn't misplaced his wallet, Cato said, none of this would have happened. But that didn't stop him finding enough money, before they trailed back through the streets, to buy a bottle of white rum.

Back home in his hammock, it didn't take Cato long either to drop off to sleep. He'd hardly started on the bottle and he was gone. The last thing he said before his eyes closed was, 'Yur mudder was a pretty gyal. That Mary-Jane – a real pretty gyal.'

What Mary-Jane? Kid thought. My mother's name was Kath. But he kept his mouth shut. It wasn't worth the bother. Cato wouldn't hear him. He was already snoring.

Kid leant over the balcony. Out there in the night he could hear the throbbing drums of punta rock, which reminded him of Night Falls Lodge. He'd been in the wrong place then, following the wrong trail, and he was in the wrong place now. His father couldn't even figure out which of the women in his life had been Kid's mother. He'd got them in a muddle. Didn't know one from the other. So much for a wedding certificate. So much even for a feather hat! How many wives had Cato had? How many mothers had fathered his children? And how many other children were there, looking just like him?

Next morning, Cato wanted Kid to go to the bank to draw out money to buy some food. He'd do it himself, he said, but since the disappearance of his wallet he had a temporary cash-flow problem.

'Ai pay yu back later,' he said, 'when Ai got tings sorted out.'

Kid drew out some money, but he knew there'd be no later. It came as no surprise to him that, as soon as he had cash in his pocket, his father was off. He had calls to make, Cato said. Business deals to attend to. He'd be back in an hour. He'd see Kid at the house.

Kid walked back on his own. He hadn't even been here for one day, but he knew he'd had enough. He climbed the stairs, kicked last night's rum bottle – which was empty now – out of the way and flung himself into the hammock. After an hour his father hadn't returned. Kid fetched his rucksack, packed it and returned to the hammock. When, after another hour, his father still hadn't returned, he left.

Kid didn't even write a note. He was too angry for anything like that. Instead he left behind his parents' photograph on their wedding day – which he didn't care if he never saw again – to remind Cato which woman was his mother.

'You win,' he said, taking a last look at the two of them together side by side.' You said my father was a man I wouldn't want to know. And you were right.'

32

GO SLOW

The water terminal building on Haulover Creek was heaving with a throng of people wanting to get out to the cayes. Kid bought a ticket and boarded the first water-taxi leaving. The sky was full of clouds as the boat nosed its way past the old warehouses, and a squally wind came up, shaking palms along the waterfront. Kid watched the shoreline in case his father came looking for him. He'd chosen a seat at the front, looking forwards, not back, because he couldn't get away fast enough.

The quays and warehouses fell behind as the boat eased out into open waters, bucking and bobbing like a swimmer in a storm. The pilot, seated above the covered cabin like a soldier at his look-out post, opened out the throttle. Immediately the boat began to slice a path through the choppy waves, sending spray flying right down the deck. People were thrown about and Kid was soaked.

If the voyage out to Caye Caulker was going to be a rough one, he decided, it was a small price to pay. Rain started beating down, but he didn't care. Tarpaulins were handed out for those passengers who hadn't found seats in the cabin area, and Kid huddled under one, listening to drops as big as pebbles beating out a rhythm like a tune on a steel drum.

For a while, all Kid could see was the edge of the boat and the sea pitted with rain. But when the downpour stopped, he emerged from the tarpaulin to find that the brown waters of Belize City had been replaced by clear, deep blue waters. In the distance he could see two tiny islands that seemed to be floating, one just big enough for a house, the other for a single palm. He wondered what it was like living on those dots of islands with nothing but ocean for company.

It rained a couple more times, and the tarpaulin had to come out again. But it never lasted long and finally the tarpaulin became a shelter from the hot sun. All around Kid, people were in holiday mode. But not him. He could feel his father's presence reaching out for him. Even when he couldn't see Belize City anymore, he could feel him trying to draw him back.

Finally Caye Caulker came into view – a long, flat island covered with palms and mangroves, surrounded by an astonishingly bright turquoise sea. A bustling waterfront appeared, along with wooden beach-front shacks, docks, boats and flocks of pelicans. A smell of beach barbecues was in the air, and Kid heard snatches of music and laughter.

People stood up in the boat to get a better view as the pilot steered towards the water-taxi dock and moored for them to disembark. Kid was first off the boat, pushing past the others as if he still couldn't put enough distance between himself and his father. A throng of people waited to offer him golf-cart rides, rooms for the night, help with luggage and cheap meals out. But he pushed past them too, hit the sandy shoreline and started along it, heading away from the water-taxi terminal.

Somewhere on this island, according to Snow's letter, were Kid's friends. But he wasn't ready for them yet. He passed a row of thatched cabanas, followed by a waterfront restaurant, a collection of beach bars and a hotel garden full of palm trees and exotic flowers. The sun was high and bright, the island picture-postcard perfect. It was a place for rest. A place for fun. A place for chilling out. But something drove Kid on, unable to stop.

'Wha' de hurry?' a voice called out as Kid charged

past. 'On de Caulker, wi go slow.'

Kid didn't even bother to look round at the man, who'd stopped raking the sand to watch him, shaking his head in disbelief. He pressed on, telling himself that he couldn't hang about. He had to put the past behind him. It was the way he'd always lived his life, sofa after sofa and flat after flat, and now he had to do it again.

Finally Kid left the built-up part of the island and entered a deep green area of mangroves. The path he'd been following disappeared and he didn't know which way to go. For a while he forced himself on. But his reasons for hurrying began to fade. The sun was hot. He was running with sweat. His rucksack dug into his shoulders. Why was he doing this? After all, as he well knew, no distance between himself and Cato could ever be enough.

Kid stopped at last, dug down in his rucksack, pulled out his mother's hat and nursed it in his arms as if it was a teddy-bear. He could feel her hurt. It was his hurt too. She'd hoped for a husband here in Belize, just as Kid had been hoping to find a father. They'd both hoped to find love – but Marcus Aurelius Cato was what they'd found instead.

The day was almost over by the time Kid returned to the village part of the island, ready to dig out Snow's letter and track down his friends. He bought a burger, smothered it in Marie Sharpe's sauce and was just walking away with it when a voice said, 'They're good, aren't they?'

Kid turned round. Hal stood behind him, grinning. At least, the voice was Hal's, but the hair had grown, the skin was brown and the stocky body had lost a tonne of weight.

'What you doing, creeping up on me?' Kid said.

'And what are *you* doing, buying burgers from Pirates' without including us?' parried Hal.

They both laughed. Hal said that Pirates' Burger Joint was the best in the world and Kid, as an expert on burgers, said he had to agree. They walked together along the waterfront, and Kid asked where Hal was staying, and if any beds were going. Hal said there'd always be a hammock in the garden if there weren't any beds in the house, but that people came and went all the time, so there were bound to be free ones tomorrow if there weren't tonight.

The hostel was set back behind a lovely sprawling beach-garden, full of hammocks, swings and palms. A pale blue *palapa* thatched with wispy dried grasses stood at one end of it, its legs planted in the sea, and the hostel stood at the other, a spider's web of decks, balconies and staircases, all decorated in bright colours with an exotic mural of an emerald-green sea goddess painted along the front wall.

Kid had scarcely had time to take it in, however, before Hal said, 'Look who I've got here . . .'

Everybody looked up from whatever they were doing. Tilda and Al sat on the veranda, a pack of cards between them. Joanne was lounging on the palapa with Jack, the black-haired Goth look gone for ever, bleached out by the sun, both reading books. Wallace was tanning his body on the dock with his headphones on.

Everybody leapt up, shrieking. But Snow was the first one to get to Kid. Snow, who'd been taking in her washing from the second-floor balcony, leapt over it, down the stairs, over the banister, down a second flight of stairs and across the veranda, crying, 'Oh my God! I don't believe it! Kid, *it's you!*'

Kid found himself being hugged by everyone, and slapped on the back. Everybody was thinner than last time he'd seen them. It wasn't just Hal. They were more shaggy-haired and wearing far fewer clothes. Some of the girls wore make-up, some of the boys sported ragged bits of beards and everybody's hair was bleached by the sun. But despite the beach-bum look, they were the same old team, and everybody had a story to tell and questions they wanted to ask – and they all wanted to do it at the same time.

Before they could ask anything, however, a voice

called down from the first-floor balcony, where the owner of the hostel had her office, that if the new boy with a rucksack wanted a bed for the night he'd better book it quick.

The owner's name was Elena. Kid went upstairs to find himself confronted by a tall, brown-skinned woman in an emerald-green bikini, who bore a remarkable resemblance to the sea goddess painted on her front wall. Her hair looked like golden sea-weed and smelt of a heady mixture of flowers and salt. Her smile was warm, but there was a definite warning in her eyes that nobody crossed her and came out alive. She was surrounded by a pack of dogs who all took to Kid. She said she liked a man who could be trusted by dogs and he almost wondered if she was flirting with him, until he worked out that she had to be at least twenty years older than him.

Kid spent the rest of the day either playing with Elena's dogs or sitting in the Sports Bar next door to the hostel, catching up on everybody's news. Apparently both teams' projects had been a huge success. There had even been a ceremony to thank them all. It had been attended by one of Belize's Channel 7 television news teams, and a handful of dignitaries had been helicoptered in to officially open the bunkhouse.

Some of them had been real wimps, Al said, worrying about snakes and *xateros* and things like that. But all of them had agreed that the volunteers from Wide-World Treks had done a wonderful job, playing a part in protecting one of the world's last great wildernesses.

'They weren't so impressed with our living conditions, though,' Joanne said. 'We thought we'd really smartened up the camp for the occasion, but the word they used to describe it was primitive. They were shocked at the way we'd had to live. I couldn't see why at the time, but I suppose I can now that I'm back in the land of chocolate cake and cocktails on the beach. I mean, our camp was home, and we were really proud of it. But it was still pretty basic. You have to admit that.'

Kid said that he was admitting no such thing. He'd missed the camp too much to have a word said against it. But then he'd missed the whole of Chiquibul. A sigh ran round the group as everybody remembered what they missed most. Howler monkeys got a mention, and so did the coolness of the early morning, with mist between the trees. Evening swims in the Rio Blanco were high on everybody's list, and everybody agreed that moonlight shining down on to the forest floor was an unforgettable sight.

'Nothing will ever be the same,' said Jack.

'I'll certainly never be the same,' said Hal – and everyone agreed, because they all knew they'd changed.

People started talking about what they'd do next. Snow was going to college as her parents had always wanted, but she intended to become an environmental scientist, which definitely wasn't on their list of approved careers. Hal was going back to the family farm, but the choice hadn't been automatic, and it hadn't been easy either. Jack was going to write a novel about his experiences in Belize. Al was going home for a good sleep. Joanne was in love with Sam from the boundary-cutting team, who was on a placement now and she was hoping to go and join him. Wallace wanted to go travelling round South America. See if he could meet up with Cassie and Doc Rose.

And what about Kid, they all wanted to know.

Kid didn't know what to say. In the distance he could hear the muffled roar of the reef. Beyond it he knew the sea was deep and unpredictable, and its currents were strong. But here, within its protective arm, he felt untouchable.

'I'm on holiday,' he said. 'I have a bed. I have my friends – at least I do for the next few days, until you guys leave. And, best of all, I've slowed down. And that's good enough for now.'

33

DUENDE

It was only later that night – sitting on the palapa with Hal and Snow – that Kid finally opened up about his placement. The island seemed to be alive with light, from the electric rays glowing beneath the surface of the water, to the lanterns hanging in the palm trees in the hostel garden, making it look like a stage for some play – Shakespeare's *Tempest*, or something like that.

Kid told them about Reuben and Lydia, about the school, Teacher Betty and his total inability to instil information into small children. He told them Joseph's story about the founding of the village, and he told them how beautiful Blue Bank Springs was with the Maya Mountains in the distance and the jungle all around it. He told them about Renaldo with his endless asking Kid's name. He even told them about the hurricane shelter, and the shameful circumstances under which he'd heard paranda music for the first time.

But he didn't tell them about Xa-an, or say anything about the sweat-house by the river where she'd restored him to health. And he didn't tell them about Renata. How could a person like her be turned into a traveller's tale?

When Kid had finished, Hal said he wished he'd chosen to do a placement too. 'You make me wish I wasn't going home,' he said. 'And that's saying something.'

Snow didn't say a thing. Only later, when Hal had gone to bed, did she ask, quietly, 'What went wrong?'

Kid blushed. He'd thought he'd hidden it so well. 'Who says anything went wrong?' he said.

'You don't need to pretend,' Snow said. 'I could tell when you arrived that something had happened. You're different.'

Kid could have fobbed her off, saying they all were different now. But instead he admitted defeat. 'There was a girl . . .' he said, and it all came out, starting that first day in Blue Bank Springs and ending with his father.

Snow was thrilled to learn he'd found himself a father, and wanted to know more. But that could wait for later. It was the girl she was most interested in. 'So what's her name?' she wanted to know.

'It doesn't matter,' Kid replied. 'She was pleased to see the back of me. It was she who talked me into leaving, saying it would be good for me. But she didn't even come to say goodbye.'

'Perhaps she didn't really want you to leave,' Snow said. 'Have you thought about that? Perhaps she only told you to because she thought it would be good for you.'

Kid said he didn't want to talk about it any more. He said goodnight to Snow and went up to bed. But he hardly slept – and it wasn't a dormitory full of snoring bodies that kept him awake, or an electric fan moaning like a tropical storm. It was Snow's words ringing in his head.

Early next morning, Kid dressed and left the hostel before anyone else was up. The sun hadn't yet risen, but the sky was lightening. He headed along the empty waterfront, past the water-taxi terminal and the rustic beach-huts built on stilts, on until he reached the mangroves. Here he stopped to watch the sun rise out of the water in a great, blazing ball of yellow light, then carried on again as if Snow's words, and the questions that they raised, were driving him.

Could Renata really not have wanted him to leave, he asked himself, like Snow had said? And had doing so been good for him? What had he learned by going with his father? And what about his journey all the way from England? Had his time here in the trees made a difference to his life? Could he see things now with clearer eyes? Was he any closer to finding a place in the world that he could call home? And if he left tomorrow, what would he take away with him?

All Kid's friends were taking away something from Belize – a different attitude, a changed ambition, a new hope for the future, even a renewed appreciation of what they had at home.

'But what about me?' Kid asked himself. 'What do I have?'

And the answer was that he didn't know.

By now Kid had long since left the inhabited part of the island and entered an area of dense forest set back from the shoreline. Twisted roots stretched across his path and butterflies danced from tree to tree, as large and bright as any he'd seen in the jungle. It was good to be back amongst trees again. Good to slot back into jungle-trekking mode, eyes peeled for snakes or the sorts of plants, like poisonwood, which he knew not to touch.

Kid glimpsed a rough-skinned iguana with pointy scales running down its spine, and startled a spoonbill, which rose on huge pink wings and swept away.

He had reached the southernmost tip of the island now, and was picking his way round a series of swampy pools. There were no houses here, no docks or palapas or other signs of human habitation, so it came as a surprise when a figure appeared ahead of him, lit up by sunlight breaking through the trees.

At first Kid thought the figure was of a child but, as he drew closer, he saw a little man. 'Good morning,' he began but the man raised a hand to silence him.

'I wouldn't come this way, if I were you,' he whispered. 'There's a croc on the track – and he's a big un too.'

Unable to see the croc, Kid froze on the spot. The man tiptoed over, finger to his lips, and led him on a woven path between the trees, pushing through the undergrowth, his footfall silent, taking care that not a single leaf should rustle. Kid could have sworn he heard a drum beating somewhere, but it could have been his heart; he wasn't sure.

'Thanks,' he said when the little old man finally let go of him, saying he'd be all right from here.

The little man looked at him. His face was brown and shiny, his teeth stained yellow and his eyes flecked with sunlight, like dots of gold in a river bed.

'Home's not a place,' he suddenly said, as if he could read Kid's mind and knew how empty he felt.

'It's a state of mind. The trees won't leave you, when you go. They're a way of life that's all your own. They're what you take everywhere you go. Once you've lived amongst them, you'll always flourish in their shade. However far you travel, they'll always be your home.'

34

KID'S BIG BREAK

How the little man slipped away, disappearing without Kid actually seeing him going, he could never afterwards explain. But if that figure out of legend – that guardian of the forest known as the *Duende* – had met Kid that day, he couldn't have felt more changed. And perhaps they had met. Who could say? Perhaps saving him from the croc had been the *Duende*'s way of saying thanks, as if Kid's efforts out in Chiquibul had been noticed and appreciated. Or perhaps the thanks were in the words he'd said.

Kid headed back towards the village. He didn't quite know what had happened back there, but he felt as if he'd had his special ceremony too – his moment in the limelight, and it mightn't have been recorded on Belize's Channel 5 TV, but who cared about that?

Returning to the hostel, he found everybody up

314

for what was to be their last full day together, keen to make the most of their precious time. He tried telling them what had happened to him, but no one was listening. For those going on to Spanish language school in Guatemala there were bus timetables to be checked, and for those flying home, there were emails to be sent, making last-minute arrangements for being picked up at the other end.

The internet access was in Elena's office. Everybody piled in, including Kid who didn't have any emails to send, but didn't want to be left out. Much to his surprise, he found a couple of messages in his inbox. The first was from Craig, warning him, that a man who claimed to be his father had nicked his address and was heading his way.

'No way would I have given him your details,' Craig wrote, 'not without permission. But, oddly enough, he's not the only one interested in you. The other day we had a visit from some local taxi driver offering you a job. She wants you to teach her daughter English, would you believe. She seems to think you and her might hit it off. Her name's Carmelita, by the way. The daughter, that is. The driver's name is Taxi-May.'

Kid laughed when he read that. But he didn't laugh when he read the second email. It came from Nadine. She didn't ask how he was, or even if he was still alive, just said she'd been feeling guilty ever since he'd left England, and lonely too since she and Kyle had split up, and if he wanted to come back, he could always make a home with her.

Yeah right, thought Kid, until the next boyfriend comes along.

But it was the last part of the message that really got to him. 'It's an open offer,' Nadine wrote. 'Any time. After all, apart from your grandmother, I'm the nearest you've got to a relative.'

Kid had to look away after reading that, because it was true – and how grim was that?

'You all right?' said Elena who noticed something in his face.

'I'm fine,' Kid said.

After finishing their emails, everybody went down to their favourite beach, known as the Split, where Caye Caulker had been cut in half during a hurricane. The water was deep here, and good for swimming, and everybody's favourite bar was here too – the Lazy Lizard, where iguanas lined up to bathe in the noonday sun.

Everybody lounged about, tried their hands at snorkelling, swam, stretched out in the sun, drank piña coladas made from fresh pineapple, and played with Elena's dogs, who'd taken to following Kid in particular everywhere he went.

He imagined staying on after the others had left. Why not, he asked himself. What else was he going to do? There'd be no Spanish language school for him, or backpacking round South America, and he definitely wasn't planning on returning to Blue Bank Springs, not after the fool he'd made of himself there. And as for Nadine's offer – even if Kid ran out of money, no way would he go back there.

Kid imagined finding a beach-bum's job and raking the sand, or learning to dive properly and helping out on the dive-boats. When the holiday season was over, he could head back to San Ignacio and take up Taxi-May's offer of teaching Carmelita English. Or perhaps he could even persuade Craig and Jasmine that they needed a Boy Friday to do the chores for them.

At the end of the afternoon, everybody sauntered back together along the shoreline. A light breeze blew a handful of flyers along the sand advertising a party that night on the north side of the island. Wallace picked one up and read it out loud, saying, 'How about it?'

But everybody had packing to do tonight, ready for an early-morning departure, and, besides, they wanted to have a last meal together in the Sports Bar, not go to some party.

At least that's what they said until Kid looked at the flyer and saw a name.

Paul Nabor.

After that, everybody *had* to go. This was someone, Kid insisted, who no way, absolutely, could be missed. 'Who's Paul Nabor?' everybody wanted to know. 'Come and find out,' Kid replied. 'You'll regret it if you don't.'

That evening, as the sun set over the Caye Caulker rooftops, everybody piled into a water-taxi to be ferried round to the north side of the island. The moon was rising as they headed up its coast. It shone across the water to a beach of pure white sand from which the sound of drumming drifted out to greet them.

The water-taxi dropped them off beside a dock illuminated by strings of lanterns and rows of flares. A fire burned on the beach, and cans of smoking incense kept mosquitoes at bay. A beach-side bar glowed in the dark like a golden shrine. The smell of barbecued food wafted across the sand while a live band sweated out a diet of punta rock.

Kid pushed his way between a crowd of dancers, heading for the bar, whose decks and balconies on different levels looked out over the ocean. His friends were dancing too, and calling for him to join them, but he held himself back. Let them boogie if they wanted. He was saving himself.

Hours later – or so it seemed to Kid – the main attraction of the night finally stepped up. His arrival came almost unheralded – a little man in a grey suit and white cowboy hat that seemed a bit too large for him, stepping up to the microphone. His face was wizened and he looked incredibly old. Could this possibly be Paul Nabor? This old man with the hooded eyelids and the thin grey moustache?

Kid experienced a sense of astonishment. Never had it crossed his mind that the owner of a voice so strong and passionate could possibly be anything but young. The man said something which Kid didn't understand, but everybody clapped and shouted, including Elena, Kid noticed, who was in the crowd as well, looking every inch the goddess in a tight red dress.

But the moment the old man started singing, Elena was forgotten. Suddenly Kid was transported back to Dangriga. It was as if he was standing in that bus terminal again, outside that music booth, captivated by a voice, wanting to know whose it was. Captivated by a song as well – which he was now hearing again, sung in the flesh.

Kid pushed to the front of the crowd, utterly entranced. Like a mystery with hidden roots the song rose out of the old man like smoke out of darkness. It was accompanied by cheers, and cries of sheer delight. Clearly Kid wasn't the only one who loved this song. The crowd started dancing, and he found himself caught up with them. It was as if something deep and dark had been uncorked and was being poured down them all. The crowd was singing along, and he sang with them. He mightn't know the words – mightn't even know the language – but it made no difference; he knew what the words meant. When Paul Nabor finished singing and announced his song's name, it came as no surprise:

'Naguya Nei'.

'I Am Moving On'.

Heading home that night beneath a ragged moon, Kid felt like a bottle of champagne fizzing with excitement at what lay ahead. Between those two magicians – the old man in the morning and this other one tonight – this was a day he'd never forget. As the south side of the island drew closer, Kid caught voices in the air and saw roll-ups glowing red on the ends of docks where people were enjoying the warm evening air.

'I've got something I want to say to you . . .'

Kid turned his head. Snow was just behind him, and there was something edgy about her. It wasn't just her voice, it was the way she was sitting.

'Can't it wait?' he said.

'It's been waiting all day,' Snow said. 'But there's

never a right minute. If I don't do it now, I might miss the chance.'

'Chance for what?' said Kid. Not that he wanted to know. For Snow was going to spoil things. He could feel it coming.

'Your chance for life,' Snow said.

'My chance for *what*?' Kid said, taken aback.

Snow explained. She'd had an email that morning from her father who'd heard about Kid and what a friend he'd been and everything he'd done for her. He reckoned that everyone deserved a chance, including Kid. To this end, he'd said that if Kid wanted to get on in life, he'd give him his support.

'Support?' Kid said.

'His money actually,' Snow said. 'You know, to help you get an education.'

Kid looked at Snow as if she were mad. An education? Only one sweet hour ago he'd been getting the only education a boy needed, courtesy of Paul Nabor.

'What are you on about?' he said.

Snow flushed. This was proving harder than she'd expected. 'I'm on about qualifications,' she said. 'A levels. Degrees. Diplomas. University. Whatever's needed to get a start in life. That's what my father's offering you.'

Kid shook his head. 'But your father doesn't

know me,' he said. 'Why would he do that?'

'Because you're my friend,' Snow said.

'But you've got lots of friends,' Kid said.

'You're the only one who saved me from a jaguar,' Snow said.

'I never saved you,' Kid said. 'There was never any danger. You know that.'

'I know I do – but my father doesn't. He thinks you saved my life.'

Kid shook his head. Dimly he was aware that Hal, on the other side of Snow, was listening in, and other people were as well. 'You mean your father would cough up all that money because of that?' he said.

'Are you saying my life's not worth it?'

Kid laughed. They both did. For a moment there the perfect evening had been in danger of being spoilt right at the end, but neither of them were going to let that happen.

The boat came in to dock, and everybody jumped ashore and headed back to the hostel for what remained of the night. Tilda and Al sneaked off together, arms around each other as if something definitely was going on there, saying it wasn't worth going to bed. Hal said even an hour's sleep was worth it and the others agreed, all except for Kid who said he reckoned he'd stay up and watch the sunrise.

Snow went up with the others. 'Let's talk again in the morning,' she said in parting. 'It's not often Dad and I see eye to eye. So think about it. This could be your big break.'

3 5

UNDER THE SHADE, I FLOURISH

Kid slept out on the palapa, rocking in one of Elena's hammocks, soothed by the sound of palm trees shaking in the night breeze. The sea washed back and forth beneath him, but Kid didn't see it. In his dreams he was back in school, pen in hand, sitting an exam which he didn't know any answers to, Teacher Betty's words ringing in his head like a funeral bell.

'It isn't fair . . . It isn't fair . . . It isn't fair . . . You English boys and girls, you have it all . . .'

Next morning Kid awoke knowing what he had to do, even though he mightn't want to. He went indoors to find people up before him, making coffee, eating breakfast, clearing out their rooms. He packed his rucksack, and hauled it downstairs to Elena's office to tell her he was leaving and to settle up. She lay sprawled across a sofa in last night's red dress.

'Yes, yes,' she said sourly when he said that he was off. 'Go, go. You're just like all the others. Quickly come and quickly gone – here for the sandy beaches, but not the hurricanes. Not the rainy season when the island's all but washed away. Not the boredom of the winter months, stuck here with no visitors. Leave your money on the table and don't slam the door. You may not have noticed, but I'm feeling fragile today.'

Kid wanted to ask about Paul Nabor. He wanted to know all about paranda and the dark way it was sung. Before he could pluck up the courage to ask anything, however, the others came pouring in, wanting to settle up too.

Elena yelled at them all to go away. She'd had enough of running a hostel, she said. She'd had enough of Caye Caulker. She'd had enough of Belize. It was a cruel country. Health, wealth, youth – it all got stripped away.

People started creeping away. Then Elena felt guilty and made them come back. They made her a black coffee and she sorted out their bills as if doing them a favour. Belize might be a cruel country, she said, but it was also full of hope. They mightn't know that, seeing it only with outsiders' eyes, but she wanted them to remember it.

'Whether for a better day, a better government or

the chance to turn our fortunes round, it's in our blood,' she said. 'Like a river rich with gold, we run with hope. It's deep down in our soil, like buried oil. It's as much our national heritage as Belikan beer – and why I'm telling you this I don't know. You're standing there wanting to go, and your water-taxi's waiting, your plane's leaving and the next backpackers are queuing to come in. Well, good for them. Good for you all.'

Elena stopped at last. Her face looked ghastly. Picking up her coffee, she downed a paracetamol. 'I've got a hangover,' she said.

Out on the balcony, Kid could see that Elena was right – the water-taxi had docked. He grabbed his rucksack and crossed the garden, waddling like a migrating turtle, the others hurrying after him. They made it on to the boat in time, but Hal left his flip-flops behind and Kid's one regret was that he never said goodbye properly to Elena's dogs.

Snow sat beside him in the stern of the boat, where his eyes were fixed on Caye Caulker, drinking it in as if he'd never see it again. She didn't ask what he'd decided to do but, realising how much she wanted to know, he told her anyway.

'If there's a cancellation, I'll fly back with you. If not I'll take the first flight I can. Some people would kill for a break like this. How can I turn it down?'

Snow touched Kid's hand as if she understood how hard this was. 'You mustn't think of this as goodbye,' she said. 'You'll be back. We both will. Our whole lives lie ahead of us. One day we'll return with our degrees to lead conservation projects of our own, and I'll be Candy and you'll be Jez. It's all a matter of having power, Kid. The power to do the things that need to be done. And education is power. I didn't know that once, but I can see it now.'

Kid was sure that she was right. But if that sort of power lay within his grasp, then why did he feel so powerless? And if his whole life lay ahead of him, then why did he feel as if everything that mattered had come to an end?

Desperately, Kid tried to find something to hold on to, something that would make sense of his leaving. And suddenly the *Duende*'s words came into his head.

'Home's not a place. It's a state of mind. The trees won't leave you, when you go. They're a way of life that's all your own. They're what you take everywhere you go. Once you've lived amongst them, you'll always flourish in their shade. However far you travel, they'll always be your home.'

Kid felt better after that. The sea turned from blue to brown and the shoreline of Belize City came into view. Slowly it drew closer until he could make out warehouses along Haulover Creek and see crowds of tourists along its quays. A boat with a brown sail went dipping past, heading out to sea, then the water-taxi nosed into the creek and that was the moment when Caye Caulker really became a thing of the past.

Kid heard the roar of traffic on the swing-bridge up ahead, and saw a new consignment of passengers waiting to embark. Their rucksacks looked new and their clothes freshly minted. Had they just come from the airport, Kid wondered. How many were bound for Elena's hostel, and what would they make of her and her of them?

Kid was the first ashore, wanting to get on with things and not to hang about. Inside the terminal building, the Spanish language school group made their goodbyes. Everybody promised to keep in email touch, or meet in England when they returned. This wasn't goodbye for ever, they promised each other as the air-conditioned tourist coach to Guatemala pulled up. They were friends for life.

The language people piled on board, still trying to shout things out and wave. But people piled in behind them and they were swallowed up. The coach began to pull away. No one could see each other any more.

'Let's get out of here,' said Wallace – big man

Wallace, shamelessly brushing tears out of his eyes and not minding who saw. 'Where are we going? Does anybody know?'

Everybody seemed to have different ideas – Joanne was all for finding a taxi, whereas Snow and Hal reckoned it would be cheaper to travel to the airport by bus. Amid the clamour of voices, Kid suddenly heard something he recognised. Something that *really* took him back.

'How yu be so mean? Ai pay yu a compliment. Ai sing yu a song. Come back. Ai speakin' to you. *Why you walkin' away from mi?*'

George the Jamaican. Kid laughed out loud. He couldn't see the man, but he could imagine the nervous tourist trying to shake him off. 'Ai speakin' to yu,' George called again. And suddenly he might have been talking to Kid.

Kid froze to the spot. Why *was* he walking away? Did he even know? Was it because some girl in Blue Bank Springs hadn't fallen in love with him? Or was it because she had? Or was it because old Cato had let him down? Or was it because Belize *was* a hard country, like Elena had said? Or was he walking away because of what he'd discovered about himself – an English boy like him, with opportunities that other people lacked, driven home by guilt?

Somewhere ahead of him, Kid could see Wallace

locating the taxi rank and waving everybody over. Luggage was being piled into the back of a minibus with sliding doors, and everybody was pushing their way in. Hal turned and looked for him. He had his old *what's Kid up to* expression on his face. Snow was in the minibus now, wedged in against the window by Star Wars Al.

'Hurry up,' called Hal, catching sight of him amid the crowd on the sidewalk.

Kid made a choice. 'You go ahead,' he called.

'What did you just say?'

'I said I'm staying.'

'You're doing *what*?'

'You heard. I'm staying.'

Hal pushed through the crowd. 'What do you mean?' he said. 'There isn't time for this. We're meant to be at the airport. Stop messing about.'

'I'm not messing about.'

'Of course you are. We can't leave you here alone.'

'Why not? I came here alone.'

The two of them stood staring at each other. Kid could see Hal struggling to grasp what was going on. 'Let me get this straight,' he said. 'When you say *you go ahead*, you mean *goodbye*. And when you say you're staying, you mean for good.'

Kid nodded. 'I'm going to start again,' he said. 'In

all this time, just like Elena said, I've only ever seen Belize with an outsider's eyes. But now I'm going to see with my own eyes. There's a whole new journey waiting to be had, and a whole new set of lessons to be learned from scratch. And they might be hard. As hard as any lessons in any school. I mightn't know where I'll end up. But it's what I've got to do.'

Hal wanted to argue, but plainly didn't know what to say. Behind him, Kid could see Snow at the minibus window, mouthing *what's going on?* He turned away. A bigger man than him would have stayed to explain that her father's offer, though kindly meant, would be better spent on someone else. And maybe Kid would be that man one day, but he wasn't yet.

Kid walked away. The throng of people on the street closed in around him. He could hear Hal calling out, 'You're making a terrible mistake.' But Hal was wrong. Kid was too young for mistakes. He'd got time on his side.

Kid headed across town, putting as much distance as possible between himself and the taxi-rank, just in case his resolve gave way. He dodged on and off sidewalks and cut across streets, horns honking at him. Only when he reached the local bus terminal, where the rattling tin-can local buses came in and out, did he allow himself to think about what he'd done. In a taxi to the airport were the members of his family, heading home without him. But then they'd always be his family, no matter what distance lay between them.

That's what families were all about.

Kid sat on a bench, wondering what to do next. Whichever bus he chose, his journey would be slow, he guessed. But then so what? Maybe in his last life he'd hurried all the time, but things were different now. That's what this new journey was all about. It was about learning lessons, and going slow. About taking time and seeing what life had to show him. Seeing it with fresh eyes.

Two buses pulled up, one bound for Cayo District, its destination San Ignacio, the other heading down to Punta Gorda on the Southern Highway, passing Blue Bank springs. Kid checked the departure times for both, then returned to his bench and sat between them, remembering what Joseph had once said:

'Before I do a thing, I always think.'

AFTERWORD

Hiking the Chiquibul Forest of Belize is a daring and challenging task, even for FCD rangers whose job it is to patrol these forests. And every time it has new surprises. In early 2008 I met Pauline in the Chiquibul Forest near an area named the Devil's Backbone. To my surprise she had hiked the farthest distance our patrols reach, and was returning back in one piece! To this day I am inspired by this feat, since the hike is long and precarious, requiring stamina, rigor and, above all, a strong determined body.

The Chiquibul Forest faces several threats ranging from farming and xate extraction to poaching and looting. To reclaim its integrity several interventions are in place, and using an adaptive management technique we are constantly on the search for new ideas and partnerships. Pauline had been convinced that the gap-year experience currently underway in the Chiquibul Forest was making a difference in the protection of the forest, and also to the lives of the young volunteers.

The volunteers had been building an observation post for the Belizean military forces by the foothills of the Maya Mountains, nearby the Guatemalan border. Since its construction the presence of forces has curbed illegal farming in that area, yet the Chiquibul Forest remains under constant threats. At FCD we are strong believers that everyone can make a difference protecting wilderness areas. It is not only moral to do so, but the survival of forests will make the planet a better place for human life. Perhaps recognising that reality and being a part of that change is what also makes a change to the lives of gap-year volunteers.

The book written by Pauline, *In the Trees*, brings out this spirit of change. I hope that as you read this book it also motivates you to realise the changes that people like you can make on Earth even though it would seem that we are worlds apart.

Rafael Manzanero
Executive Director
Friends for Conservation and Development
(FCD)

Acknowledgements

For years I'd dreamt of writing a novel for young teenagers about the gap year experience. However, I had no idea what I was letting myself in for when, funded by the Authors' Foundation and the Arts Council, I went out to Belize to research the phenomenon for myself. Belize is a truly beautiful country, but it's not for the faint-hearted. Trekking through the Chiquibul Forest was the most challenging thing I'd ever done, but it was worth it to see at first hand the tragedy of despoliation taking place there, and the efforts being made by young volunteers, many straight from school, to stem the tide.

I was so proud of the young people I met out there, and all that they were achieving. The forest was fabulous – as indeed was the whole of Belize, with its great natural beauty, wonderful people and cultural diversity – and I returned home to England determined to write a book that would do justice to all that I'd seen. I made some good friends out in Belize, and would like to thank them for all their help. I would also like to thank the people here who believed in my project when it was still only half-formed, and helped make it a reality.

They include my agent, Laura Cecil, and my editor, Julia Heydon-Wells, who saw potential when all I had was a rough idea, and Emily Hardy, to whom fell the task of keeping control of my wayward manuscript; Adrian Johnson and the Arts Council; also my sponsors at the Authors' Foundation, who jointly helped fund my research project; my husband, children and brother, who held the fort back at home when all sorts of dramas blew up during my absence.

In addition I'd like to thank Rob Murray-John, who arranged for me to meet volunteers out in the jungle; Greg Coe, to whom fell the unenviable task of getting me out to them and back again; and Jen Mullier, who made the best triple-chocolate cake of my life and, more importantly, loaned me her mosquito net. I'd also like to thank the two remarkable groups of young Trekforce volunteers that I met out there, and their leaders, Sully and Katie, who welcomed me so openly into their midst and made me feel so proud of them.

Thank you also to Rafael Manzanero, the Executive Director of Belize's Friends for Conservation & Development, whom I met out in the wonderful Chiquibul Forest Reserve and has kindly written an afterword for this book; to Pablo and his family down in Toledo District, who offered me hospitality, friendship and an example of dignity and open-heartedness which will remain with me for ever; to Laura

Longsworth who talked to me about the Belizean people being full of hope, and her sister, Zee Edgell, who brought the two of us together; to Luciana Essenziale and Michael Joseph, who offered me friendship and hospitality on Caye Caulker; and to Peter Aldag, formerly of Caye Caulker, who sent me photographs of Paul Nabor at his beach resort, Driftwood, where I spent a memorable last night of my trip.

In particular, however, I'd like to thank Idris, who graciously accompanied his mother around Belize for six weeks without a word of complaint. The original gap year adventure that inspired me all those years ago was his, and so is the song whose words are reproduced on p. 156. Twelve kilometres out in the jungle he wrote these words and put them to music. We really were out 'in the trees', not another soul around, the ground beneath our hammocks covered with fresh jaguar prints. Idris called his song 'Paradise'. No other name would have done.